I'll Never Talk
Erotic Tales of Defiant Men

Jardonn Smith

I'll Never Talk
Erotic Tales of Defiant Men

Published by The Nazca Plains Corporation
Las Vegas, Nevada
2006

ISBN: 1-887895-72-8

Published by

The Nazca Plains Corporation ®
4640 Paradise Rd, Suite 141
Las Vegas NV 89109-8000

PUBLISHER'S NOTE
I'll Never Talk is a work of fiction created wholly by the Jardonn
Smith's imagination. All characters are fictional and any resem-
blance to any persons living or deceased is purely by accident.
No portion of this book reflects any real person or events.

Cover Art by Baron
Editor, Blake Stephens

DEDICATION

Dedicated to all soldiers who signed up for one fight
but were sent to another.

I'll Never Talk
Erotic Tales of Defiant Men

Jardonn Smith

CONTENTS

GERMANICUS DIVINE

What is the threshold of pain a man can endure? How far is he willing or able to go in order to maintain his integrity, his masculinity or even his sanity?

I don't know who killed Germanicus. I loved him, as we all did, but this is the Roman tradition. All slaves and household servants are put to torture. This is how the mysterious death of a beloved public figure is solved and the rabble appeased.

Germanicus was adored by many. In fact, he was worshiped nearly as a god, both for his heroic generalship of the Roman Legions and his familial connection to divine Augustus himself.

I was in charge of the stables. Born into this servitude of the Claudian family, I replaced my father upon his death. Germanicus chose me for my strong back and gentle nature with his animals. He treated me not as a slave, but as a fellow human being, respecting me for my knowledge and judgment of horses.

None of us could save him. Not even the endless entourage of purveyors of medical knowledge could reverse the inevitable. We all watched day after day in horror and sorrow, as he slowly slipped away from us. Poisoned he was. It is my theory and I will take it to my grave.

They started me on the stretch rack - that hideous ripper of joints, tendons and muscles. A rather ingenious device it is, admirable for its simplistic mechanics and brutal effectiveness.

I was stripped naked. The Romans always torture their victims in the nude, as this is part of the humiliation process - male or female, it does not matter. All defenses are removed. Placed chest up to lie flat on the horizontal table, my ankles were locked into wooden stocks, while my wrists were bound with ropes. The other ends of the ropes were wrapped around a solid wood axle, which was also horizontal and parallel to the head end of the table. Two wheels attached to either side of the axle contained tiny saw tooth gears, which allowed my tormentors to adjust and lock the rack at any tension they desired.

They were kind to me during the preparation for my torture. Even after I was secured flat on the rack, with wrists roped and arms pulled parallel to one another beyond my head, they asked me to confess. They claimed they didn't want to hurt me and that I could prevent my suffering, but I knew this was a lie. Confession meant death, which now wouldn't seem such a bad thing. Maybe that's what they meant - just get it over with.

The reality is that the Romans are not satisfied with the unholy screams that come from a man being stretched. Their appetites aren't even appeased by the first hideous sounds coming from the man's body, such as when tendons start to pull apart and joints crack. No, in between they like to give you rest periods. The tension of stretching is lessened just enough to keep your form together and this is when they do things to your body.

The unimaginative ones like to pound on you with their fists. They are especially fond of pulverizing the belly, knowing full well that it is stretched to capacity and there's nothing but muscle there to protect it.

This is how they test a man's strength. Plus, it keeps them from smashing bones, which might cause irreparable punctures to vital organs before you have been persuaded to talk. I received plenty of punches to my belly. It was a strong, manly sight before the ordeal began. Thankfully, I cannot see it too well now and really would prefer not to know what is left of it. One of them came up with a clever idea. He took his thumb and pointed it into my stretched navel, and then he started pressing down with all the strength in his massive forearm. He dug the digit in so deep I thought he would run me through, but I didn't scream on that one. No, I just sucked in my middle section to make it as flat as I could, all the while grunting and groaning with masculine sounds of resolve.

This belly button impalement sent shockwaves throughout my groin and for that reason my penis began to stir, which leads us to the more imaginative activities to take place during my rest periods.

The Romans seem to have an infatuation with the phallus. They enjoy forcing it to perform, even though the owner doesn't necessarily want it to do so. I don't know how many times I was coerced into orgasm. They would manipulate my penis with their hands. They would take it into their mouths and orally stimulate it to orgasm. They even brought in some servant girls and let them use it as a tool to bring orgasm to themselves. Just another test of endurance it was and I guess I passed - not that it did me any good, but I can't say I did not enjoy it. At least it was a temporary respite from the agony of being stretched.

Firing volleys of manly sperm into the Romans' mouths or any other orifice they could find for me was my only weapon. I recall several occasions where they were nearly gagged, either from my incredible size or massive volume of orgasmic fluids, I couldn't tell which. Either way, it was the only satisfaction I got from the entire episode. At least they knew they were dealing with a fine specimen of masculine strength.

So, the pattern was established. They'd stretch me until something snapped, then they'd loosen the rack a bit and punch my belly, spear the navel and milk my penis in all the above mentioned methods.

I never gave in - never said what they wanted to hear, because I was waiting. I had to know if a certain man would come to visit me in my private room of hell. Thus, my incentive to survive was this singular thought - my motivation:

Yes, I do know who killed Germanicus. He is a man whose false suspicions and paranoia knows no bounds. He will stop at nothing to protect his power and any person with lineage to Augustus is a threat to him, especially if this person's popularity outshines his own. His name is Tiberius, the Emperor of Rome himself. Until he arrives I will say nothing.

Of course, he did come to me. He had to know if I was clever enough to figure him out, and if so, what my intentions might be. His methods were brutal beyond words.

The punches inflicted upon me by his bony fists showed no regard for bone, as he ruthlessly pounded on my expanded chest. Ribs were cracked and the sternum battered. I spoke no words, only cries and groans of unholy agony, as he wailed on my stretched and defenseless body for countless minutes.

The other Romans stood quietly awed at my defiance. Even they seemed impressed by my show of strength, as they watched my once manly physique turned into a bruised and bloody pulp. Yes, he savagely pounded my face, probably beyond recognition, before he finally tired. Once he did and the beatings stopped, I gasped and uttered the only words I would say throughout the entire ordeal.

With my broken, twisted mouth I exclaimed, "YOU killed Germanicus. His blood is on your hands and everyone will know."

The astonished brightness of his eyes told me my remarks were true. No matter that Germanicus was the son of his brother; no matter that Tiberius had adopted the young man as his own son after the death of that brother. His jealousy and unfounded mistrust had coerced him into this irrational act, perpetrated with logical forethought and planning.

You see, my friends, he couldn't kill his nephew outright. No trumped up charges would be sufficient to convince the throngs that Germanicus deserved to die. The love and respect he enjoyed shielded him from such a fate, and so, taking lessons from his treacherous mother, who had successfully played this game many times before, Tiberius sent spies into the household as servants. First, they put curses throughout the home. Then, they poisoned his food ever so slightly day after day, until sufficient amounts were absorbed to bring about the irreversible end to this kind, loyal and heroic man.

Tiberius had his answer. I was clever enough to be a threat and witnesses had heard my accusations.

He ordered me to be whipped, and then gleefully stood by to observe my carving on the rack. The Romans ripped my flesh to shreds. My senses felt, saw, heard and even smelled the skin, as it was savagely sliced into so many pieces of raw meat. Then, I was crucified – publicly, of course, which is the Roman way. This serves two purposes - it appeases the public, who are allowed to mock and ridicule me, as my broken, bloodied body is displayed naked before them; and, as a warning and reminder to any others who might be entertaining thoughts of committing such a crime themselves.

The message is quite clear: Here before you is the murderer, who so ruthlessly took the life of our beloved Germanicus. See what happens to any who commit such a foul and heinous deed.

I must admit, Tiberius thought of everything. The Romans who tortured me were given the option of committing suicide or suffering their own executions. Plus, the words I spoke were my last, because my tongue was unceremoniously ripped from my mouth.

They didn't use spikes to hammer me to the cross. Ropes were used, as this would prolong my suffering and demise. I doubt I would have felt the spikes anyway, because my body - what is left of it - was numbed from the tearing of their whip in to flesh and muscle, which severed most of my nerve endings.

What I did feel occurred about an hour ago, as the beginnings of daylight pierced the horizon. Two Romans approached and, producing one of those metal spikes, proceeded to insert the pointed dagger like tip into my belly button. While one man held the spike, the other man professionally pounded its head with his mallet, driving the long tool completely through my navel and out the backside. I could hear the penetrating spike striking into the wood of the cross, until the head of it filled the hole of my belly button, where it now remains.

The initial pain from this final insult quickly vanished, as it was replaced by an unexplained rush of incredible masculinity. Every muscle of my abdominal cavity flexed and tensed in a natural, defensive reaction and I felt like the strongest man ever to grace this earth. Despite my crucifixion torture, I expanded the chest with each devastating whack of mallet on nail head, as my belly flattened to absorb and even invite the horrendous spike into me deeper. The clanking of metal on metal, coupled with the shockwaves reverberating throughout my belly and groin, drove me to a peculiar, ecstatic madness. My penis reacted in conjunction with the impalement. It instantly swelled with blood and snarled at my tormentors, mocking them with pre-orgasmic ooze.

The sun has set and risen two times since my useless body ascended on this cross. With daylight, the rabble has returned to marvel at my glorious manhood. The penis remains erect. It is truly a magnificent sight - so powerful, as it pulsates and penetrates the air. Few in the crowd can deny this. These oglers should consider themselves fortunate for the opportunity to observe the mighty phallus. It is all that remains of me. Apparently, the Romans admired the beauty of this manly organ so much they spared it the mutilation of their whip.

It is the final image I will observe in this world.

I will gladly journey to the next, because I know the future. History will be kind to those I love. They will become divine gods, while those I despise will suffer the agonies of hell for eternity.

Tank Books

WATER
Part One – In the Confines

There was a time when I would have cut Bart Baker's throat had I gotten the chance. I would have cracked open his head, gutted him, or any other method of life-ending measures – at one time, had I gotten the chance.

The problem with Bart? He was a bully. This is a term I use in its worst possible meaning, because the man known as Sergeant Bart Baker was a bully who had been given a position of authority – a power he used and abused to turn our world of daily routine on its head.

I had done it before, you know, taking a man's life. That fellow deserved exactly what he got from me and it was a cinch to do him in, but that was on the outside, which put me on the inside.

Penitentiary existence in the pre-Bart days wasn't so bad for Jack and me, in so far as a lifetime of confinement can be put into a positive light. Initially, of course, that was not the case. Establishing myself into the pecking order was pure hell, because once you're thrown into an internalized society of killers, arsonists, rapists and robbers, it's up to you as to what role you play and for newbies there are but three choices – top, bottom or too crazy to be messed with.

The thought of pretending to be a madman never occurred to me, which is just as well because I never could have played that game successfully for 30, 40, 50, hell, maybe 60 years. The thought of having a guy's schlong rammed up my keister was, for me, a "no fucking way that'll happen" scenario, so that left choice number one. But in order to be a number one, a fellow's got to prove himself worthy, which means he gets the crap beaten out of him before being manhandled like a number two.

They got me on my third day there, in the showers, nine versus one. Of course, I rebuffed their leader's advances, which began the assault of fists and feet. After the beating, nine cocks and plenty of soap not only took my virginity, but also my ability to walk for about a week. All I could do was shuffle along like a 90-year-old, arthritic cripple.

Reflecting on it now, I'd have to say it was a small price to pay, although at the time I didn't think so. Since I never screamed like a woman; or begged them to stop; or bartered to join their gang; or pretended that I liked them or what they were doing to me, those men decided I wasn't worth the effort it would take to break me in. They knew I would fight them every time, so an unsaid truce was made. They'd leave me alone and I'd ignore their illicit activities.

Better yet, word got out that I was cool. This meant the other kings of the pen would also let me be, as long as I looked the other way. So, no longer a newbie, I became part of the smartest segment of penitentiary society, the no-names, those who never caused any trouble for inmates or guards. We were there to do our time peaceably and be done with it.

Jack, full name Jack Jacobson, was also part of that society, after having been initiated to it in the same manner as I had. Jack's assignment to become my new cell mate changed everything and it all came about because my old cell mate didn't like me. It's not that I was a son of a bitch to live with; it's just that I had no interest. I despised him for his crime. It was impossible for me to show interest in a child rapist. They are not criminals. Nor are they human beings. They should not be in prison with their genitalia intact. They should not be anywhere before being castrated, for only then can they be trusted.

"No," I'd tell him every night. "I ain't gonna fuck you. No, you can't suck my dick. I want nothing to do with you. You're nothing but shit to me."

He tried every plan in the world to get me beaten to a pulp or killed outright, but none of the chiefs would break our truce, and besides, most everybody in there considered him to be the scum that he was, same as I did. After nearly two years of frustration, his transfer request was finally granted and this opened the door for Jack to enter.

As was the custom, I waited for him to address me. "Hello," he offered his hand for a shake. "Jack Jacobson, coming over from C Block."

"Welcome to A," I greeted while clasping that hand. "Max Skydance. Why'd they move you?"

"My roomie got thrown into solitary. He must be giving them all kinds of trouble, 'cause he's been gone about two weeks."

"What did he do?"

"Kicked a guard. Don't know what set him off. I wasn't around."

"They must have big plans for him. Splitting you two up for good."

"Fine with me. He's too crazy to be in general. Short fuse, you know?"

"Yeah, same here," I divulged. "My mate got so pissed off at me he put in for a transfer."

Although inmates quickly learn to stoically conceal thoughts, Jack's expression showed a hint of concern.

"Don't worry," I told him. "I'm easy-going with like-minded people, which that fella was not. Go ahead and settle in."

Men who plan on living together in one small space with two single beds move slowly, because if you're doing a 20-odd-years-to-lifetime sentence, it doesn't make sense to spill your life story in a couple of days. After all, what would you do with the remaining thousands? This is why personal questions are never asked, assuming you room with a serious human being. Each man speaks of himself in increments of his own choosing. Jack and I understood this.

Both of us had walked similar paths into the Texas prison system. Both had killed for what we considered legitimate reasons, regardless that the system saw it as premeditated, first-degree.

Jack Jacobson had an addiction to gambling, which led to dealings with bookies and loan sharks, which led to debts he could not repay, which led to the provider of those debts dispatching two of his goons to collect in blood. Jack shot them both – one dead and one crippled for life.

Self-defense, pure and simple.

Mine was an Indian thing. A question of honor. I knew my woman had gone off-reservation to a tavern just over the Texas border. She liked to drink. I could not drink. She liked to drink with other people. I could not be that other people. What I did not know, nor did she, was that a certain cowboy who frequented that tavern had no respect for women, red or otherwise. She had no business doing anything other than sleeping away her sickness, but was easily manipulated into leaving with the cowboy, who bedded her, fucked her, ripped her vagina to pieces with his fist, and beat her until she was nearly lifeless.

Seven teeth remained when she was found where he dumped

her, along a county road one-half mile inside New Mexico. I know, because I counted them. The cowboy was easy to find. This Indian did not kill him quickly. My knife was used first to slash, to wound, to incapacitate. By the time another patron exited the tavern and happened to see me and the cowboy, my knife was completing its 22nd stabbing, or at least that's what the coroner said.

Self-defense, pure and simple.

I have summarized the particulars of what took Jack and I one year to tell each another. Our anniversary of togetherness was celebrated at night, in shadows, just as every night before had been. Each of us, under our own blankets, stroking our own peckers while pretending we did not know what the other was doing.

Part Two – Getting to Know You

It was never explained to us why the United States Army took charge of our prison home, but the radical changes that resulted came about so quickly none of us had the time or energy to investigate. My opinion is that something had been found under the dirt of that complex – something the U.S. government wanted as soon as possible and with as little expense as could be finagled. Slave laborers is what we became, with each cell block working on their own project with their own commanding sergeant in charge of the activities. Sgt. Bart Baker was assigned to A Block, and according to him, lucrative awards awaited the men who finished their project first, although I had guessed the rewards were to be for Bart and his men, not any of the convicts doing the work.

He made it clear from day one that he was not to be questioned or challenged. Those who were foolish enough to test him, as we stood lined up military-style in the blazing sun of the outside yard, soon found themselves kneeling on the dirt after having received the butt end of a rifle either to their backside or gut. Half a dozen men took this abuse before everybody finally shut up.

Jack and I were smarter than that, answering "yes, sir" or "no, sir" and keeping our eyes directly forward when addressed by this man, as he paced the line challenging each of us with verbal trickery. It was the typical military approach to learn who we were and to categorize us accordingly: those who were the weak and easily dominated; those who would initially be trouble but easily broken down; those who were the ass-kissers; those who were the backstabbers (usually doubling as ass-kissers); those who might be useful because they held a position of power; and those who might be a serious threat – the cold, expressionless schemers.

Based on these verbal exchanges, Bart could only believe we were leaders or schemers, because our reaction to this situation was identical to all others. In fact, Jack and I had pretty much become one. Our bonds had grown to the point where we thought alike and talked alike. Both of us had learned long ago that the best policy was just to get through another 24-hour increment with no conflicts involving any authority figures. This new military regime changed nothing regarding our approach to serving our sentences. Jack's first parole hearing was within sight, only six years away, while mine was within seven, and even though we knew release rarely came on a man's first review, still, we had no intentions of screwing it up.

There had been no planning or forethought to any of it, but our relationship had strengthened day by day and night by night, beginning with Jack's first request to touch me. With permission granted, he pulled down the sheet and knelt on either side of my hips. His hands gently massaged my chest and belly before finding their way to my hardened cock. It is said opposites attract and I would not argue, for Jack's fascination with my Native American form and resulting hairless, darker skin was equaled by my curiosity of his European whiteness and resulting furred skin from chest to toes.

I did not stop my hands from traversing their own slow path of exploration, which ended with his erect penis encircled by my fingers. With a gingerly maneuvered reversal of his position, Jack took my cock into his mouth, while leaving his to dangle in the air above my watering lips. Our technique was completely amateurish and apprehensive, but the event, the momentous occasion, took us forward to a realm of no return. Practice would make it all better and this session of two-per-man-orgasms launched us upon our journey.

Abandoning the six-nine approach, we pleased one another with alternating, solo acts of praise heaped upon balls and cock, but inevitably oral service alone could not fulfill our desires. To remedy this, I was the instigator, starting with a tongue bath upon his extremely hair covered asshole. With my elbows hooked beneath his knees, I lifted and positioned to worship and slobber the crack. His taste was sweet – an aromatic flavor subtly hinted with masculine sweat, which spurred me to invade the inside rim with my tongue, until even that exercise left me unfulfilled.

Jack's moistened portal did not resist the head of my cock, nor the subsequent impalement from its shaft. I gently, lovingly, inch by inch pressed forward until my pelvis made contact with muscular, undulating cheeks. He knew from oral experience that my ejaculations were best achieved by slow, methodical strokes, and this entry to his asshole was no exception. In control, the length of my sturdy phallus retracted and returned with no regard to time, no deadlines for completion. The Max Skydance impaling serpent slithered into the hole, recoiled, and struck again to the deepest penetration, where a tantalizing rectal vise crushed its oozing mouth.

With a reversal of positions and roles, Jack entered me the same way; finality achieved with his most effective and rewarding motions – short, rapid-fire jabs. We never analyzed the reasons for our hidden activities, for you see, Jack and I loved one another before any of these shenanigans had ever been attempted. The physical discoveries were merely a consecration of what was already there, and no change of our daily routine, no alteration of the people in charge could ever erode these bonds, regardless of the cruelties and injustices that were to come.

I suspect Bart's superiors saw him as an effective leader who got prompt results, but in reality he was a sadistically bitter man stricken with a severe case of megalomania. Those underneath him were treated not as men, but as fodder, as tools placed at his disposal. Our project was to build a pumping station. We worked from sunrise to sunset in the August sun of southwestern Texas heat, interrupted by a thirty minute lunch brought to us on the site. Obviously, the Army was on a tight budget, because for sustenance we received one sandwich consisting of an unknown form of lunch meat, framed by two slices of plain, white bread; one bag of chips, corn or potato; and one small plastic cup of lemonade. Water would have been far preferable to the overly sour, lip pursing bile in a cup, but water was a prized commodity. It was the main ingredient used to not only control, but also to dehumanize.

We learned this the first day on site, just before being grouped into our work teams.

"Water's in short supply here, men," Bart shouted, while pacing along the line of already sweat dripping convicts. "Therefore, you will only receive sustenance when I feel you are in dire need of it. Your first week will be hard, but hopefully by next week there will be enough for everybody. Until then, we must all do our part to conserve."

It was a lie. Parked on site was a truck delivered, 1000 gallon container full of the stuff clearly visible to each of us, a vivid reminder that Sgt. Baker was in charge and that our best play was to work quickly – the only hope, to finish the project before we dropped from thirst.

My resolve that first day, as was Jack's, I'm sure, was to survive without groveling for Bart's water; because we saw the price other men had paid to receive Bart's precious possession. By midmorning most of us had removed our shirts and sweat flowed freely from our pores. Only when collapsed to the ground would a man be brought before the equally shirtless sergeant, who rested on a boulder next to the container. At his side was a metal drum of the liquid, along with his rifle, ladle and small tin cup. The hapless prisoner was forced to stand before him, as the escort of rifle toting army grunts returned to their guard duty.

"Thirsty, are ya'?" he taunted his first victim. "Well, you've got to earn a taste of my water. Strip."

Dumfounded, the man begged for relief. "Please, sir. One swallow is all I need."

"I told you to strip," Bart shouted, and the man painfully complied, removing boots, jeans and socks.

"All the way."

After dropping the underpants, he waited for his prize.

"Come closer."

As he did, Bart grabbed the man's tit and pinched it between thumb and finger. "Now, jack off."

"Oh, god, no. Please, sir, just one sip."

With a violent twist of the nipple, Bart repeated his command. "I said jack off, you worthless piece of shit."

And the desperate man did as told. Stricken with thirst, drenched in sweat, this poor soul degraded himself before the sergeant, clasping a reluctant peter with fingers and pumping back and forth. He exhausted what little energy remained, bringing himself to erection while Sgt. Baker attacked him with a two-handed, double titty-twister.

All the while, he mocked the man. "You're nothing but a beast. A beast of burden. You sweat like a pig. Smell like an ox. You're not even human, just a worthless animal. What good are you to me? If you can't work, you're not even an animal. You are what I say – a pile of shit."

The man closed his eyes. He tried to shut out the endless taunts and painful twisters, while concentrating on anything that might bring him to orgasm, but his body shut down before reaching that goal. Down to his knees he fell, then onto his face he lay unconscious. Here he remained for several minutes before Sgt. Baker finally rolled him onto his back, dribbled several portions of the ladle upon his stricken body to awaken him, then allowed one tin cup full of water to revive him.

"Now, get up and get back to work."

The man reached for his pants, but was thwarted. "No you don't. Today, you work naked. Next time you'll think twice before taking my water."

This was the game played. Some men managed to shoot their loads, receive Bart's cup, dress and return to their duty. Others went the way of the first man, forced to work in the buff on tender feet, but Jack and I did neither. We toughed it out that first day, not knowing that this exercise would be one of futility – a slow, agonizing death.

No more community meals in the dining hall, all dinners were served on trays delivered to the cells. Our drink? A one pint milk carton filled with water – soured water, because none of the milk cartons had been rinsed first. All running water was shut off in A Block. No more showers, no more toilets, our waste was deposited into one metal bucket placed inside each cell, emptied sporadically when one of the guards got around to it.

Isolated from prisoners in the other cell blocks, we couldn't know whether or not they were suffering as we were. The state governing board had been usurped by the military, so there were no inspections for sanitation; no regards as to our health and well-being; no constitutional rights pertaining to cruel and inhumane treatment; no familiar guards to hear our plight. All we saw were army grunts, day after day, night after night, along with Sgt. Bart Baker constantly bearing down upon us.

By the fifth day the situation was becoming intolerable. A Block stunk to high heaven. Little by little our bodies were losing the battle. Far more sweat was being expelled during the day than water coming in at night, and the result was a head on fire sitting atop a body exhausted and weak.

"What the hell are we going to do, Max?" Jack and I lay on our own filthy beds. Neither of us had the energy or desire to even think about our nightly routine of mutual gratification, nor had we since the ordeal began.

"We gotta kill him. Somehow, some way, we've got to kill that son of a bitch."

"Won't do us any good. They'll just replace him. Probably kill us on the spot, too."

"Well, if we can't kill him, then we've got to give in. We've got no choice. Not that it's going to do us any good. That little tin cup isn't going to help me. Won't do anything for the energy it'll take just to shoot a wad. Don't know about you, but it's doubtful I can go on much longer. I'm desperate, Jack. I say we kill him and be done with it."

There was a long silence, as we wrestled with this hopeless situation, until Jack sprang up to one elbow.

"All right. You leave it to me. I'll give bad ass Bart what he wants. I'll give him that and then some."

"What've you got in mind?" I asked, while raising myself to rest on an elbow.

"Don't worry. I won't do anything stupid. Just watch and listen. We'll just see if he's as bad as he wants us to believe."

As the next day dragged on, I began to wonder if Jack had decided against his plan. Morning passed and lunch was served, while I made a special effort to avoid him throughout, keeping my work angled so that I could watch everything he did. We were digging out a floor to be one foot below the surface of ground, but before the other men and I could shovel, Jack and those in his group had to break up rock with pick ax. Larger chunks were hand carried away by some, while those with shovels (including me) scooped up the smaller particles to be put into dumpsters.

By mid-afternoon, several men had already performed for Sgt. Baker. I glanced to see one man jacking in front of him, as Bart tightly finger-clamped the guy's tit. Behind them, another man who had just paid his penance and received the reward was still naked and crawling back, begging for another chance for another drink. This is when Jack made his move by dropping the pick ax and collapsing to the ground, but before guards could arrive to haul him up to Sgt. Bart, he rose to all fours and crawled towards the watering station.

I continued to shovel at an angle to give me a clear view when Bart said, "Well, well, look who's come begging. Finally broke down, did ya', tough guy?"

Jack positioned himself beside the man beating off, rose to stand erect on his knees and pleaded with the sergeant. "Please, sir. Just one drink. I'll do anything you say."

With a sneer, he planted the sole of his boot into Jack's chest. "Get back, you pathetic slime." He pushed Jack away, leaving him sprawled in the heated dirt. "Wait your turn, asshole."

Seeing Jack's brutal treatment started me to rush into the fray, but something told me to let it play out awhile, so I continued to shovel.

With Jack lying motionless, the other fellow shot his load, received the tiny portion of water, put on his clothes and stumbled away from the watering station.

"Private," Bart pointed to the naked man. "Get this loser back to work. He's had his fill."

As that one was hauled away, Jack rallied to once again kneel before the sergeant. "Please sir, now may I have a drink?"

"Sure. You know the routine. Lose the clothes."

He began to strip, but kept on talking. "Sir, I don't know if I can beat off without some help. Water won't quench my thirst."

"What the fuck are you talking about?"

"Please, sir. Let me drink your come. I'm the best there is. Let me show you. Please, sir."

This brought a hardy laugh of sarcasm. "Oh, I get it. A queer Jew boy. Is that what you are, Jacobson?" And again, a booted kick to the chest sent Jack sprawling, this time with the jeans and underpants pulled down to his knees. Jack lay there seeming to be unconscious, which made my blood boil. Even though I knew better, bad temper got the best of me and I rushed towards Bart Baker with shovel in hand, but stopped when Jack again rose to his feet.

"Let me suck your dick, sir. You won't regret it. I don't want any friggin' water. Just you."

"You cock sucking queer. You make me want to puke." He looked up to where I stood motionless, shovel still in hand. "What the hell do you want?" he barked.

"Nothing, sir." I dropped the tool. "It's just that... well, this man is my cell mate and I can tell you he's like nothing I've ever known. It's not a blow job, sir. It's something I can't describe. It's too good to be put into words."

Bart contemplated what he heard, looking to Jack, who tantalizingly licked his dry lips with whatever spit he could muster.

"Ain't this something? Here I got a queer Indian telling me I should let his queer, Jew boyfriend suck my dick. That's one hell of a note."

He was talking tough, but the bulge in his camouflage-panted crotch told me he was genuinely intrigued by our suggestion, so I pressed on.

"Believe me, sir. He does me every night and every night it just gets better and better. Let him show you. You won't regret it."

Sergeant Bart rubbed his chin, staring down at the tongue wagging Jack. "Get a drink Jacobson. Take all you need. Dry mouth won't do me any good."

While Jack quenched his thirst, Bart looked to me with an evil grin. "Ok, red man, we'll just see what this supposed cock sucker can do, but you're gonna be a part of it. While he's sucking on me, I want you to put that big Indian dick of yours up his ass. He's gonna have to earn the right to get me off."

Sergeant Bart remained motionless and leaning against his boulder, allowing Jack to open up the fly of his trousers.

"Slow down there, Jew boy. You get nothing 'til Crazy Horse starts fuckin' you good and hard. That's what I want to see."

"I got no spit, sir," I told him.

"Well, get a drink then, you god damned heathen."

My belly was filled and mouth satiated to replenish six days of denial. After spitting a giant goober into my hand, I gobbed it all over Jack's sweaty asshole, then produced another hocker to lubricate my cock. With Jack standing, waist bent 90 degrees, his innards were easily filled. Just as had been done countless times before, I expertly stroked to and fro, while Jack received and cuddled my dick as only he could.

"Oh, yeah," Bart moaned. "Pound that bitch's ass. Oh, man, that's beautiful. Fuck yeah, Injun, tenderize that asshole."

Sergeant Baker exposed himself with his own hand, presenting a glorious cock beautifully shaped and sized, fully charged and ready for action. Inhaling with one massive gulp, Jack moved his lips directly to the man's pelvis and crushed the dick head into the back of his throat.

"Ah, Jesus," he exclaimed as though experiencing an unknown pleasure. Bart threw back his head from the touch of an expert. Things only got better for him, as Jack slowly withdrew the lips, ruthlessly scraping inch by inch with his tongue on the underside of Bart's shaft.

"Holy shit. Jesus fucking Christ." Sergeant Bart quickly understood exactly what I'd been telling him was true, and I watched with glee as his body nearly collapsed, but a buzz behind us caused the sergeant to collect himself. All work had stopped and convicts were drifting towards our configuration to get a better look, until a shouting of guards issuing threats of "get back to your stations or we'll blast you" cleared the way for Jack and me to continue uninterrupted.

Bart returned to his ecstatic trance. He clasped both hands onto the boulder and leaned back to enjoy the ride, while Jack's expertise fulfilled our promise to him.

From this point forward, Sergeant Baker was vulnerable and Jack had two options. He could either launch a physical assault, holding Bart's cock hostage until all prisoners had quenched their thirst, or he could rearrange Bart's way of thinking with the blow job of a lifetime. Jack chose option number two. As for me, I knew my assignment, and that was to dramatically skewer Jack's asshole as I had done so many times before, giving Bart plenty of theater with which to further stimulate himself.

His pleasurable exclamations were no more. Bart locked eyes with mine, occasionally glancing down first to my point of entry, then to the mouth on his dick, while leaning motionless against the boulder and allowing Jack to work his magic.

I had silently and without warning fired my load into Jack's ass when Bart's eyes rolled to the back of his head. He clamped fingers and thumbs onto his own nipples, then violently exhaled with a pleasured moan, every muscle tensed and belly pooched outward. Jack slavishly stroked, while Bart twitched and convulsed to excrete one gob after another of his manly semen into Jack's mouth. Meanwhile, I watched and waited by pressing my quickly-fading unit into Jack's hole as deep as I could manage, only withdrawing when Bart did the same. As Sergeant Baker's moistened and drained cock was removed from the darkness of Jack's mouth and returned to glimmer in the heated daylight, Jack and I waited silently to see what the next response would be.

There was none, except for a command issued in a soft voice only we could hear. "Put on your pants. Get back to work."

While dressing, we tag teamed against him. "Sir, men work faster when they ain't dying of thirst."

"I know, Jacobson. They're looking kinda ragged."

"Sir," I joined in, "a man's skin can only take on so much dirt and sweat. If we could shower..."

"I know, I know," he interrupted. "Shut the hell up and get back to work. Everything's going to be fixed. I'll make things right, but I'm still in charge, so keep your mouths shut, ok?"

"Yes, sir," we simultaneously agreed.

Jack and I suddenly became heroes to all the men of A Block, because each of them, one by one, were escorted by Bart himself to the watering hole, where they were allowed to drink until satisfied. That evening, the showers were turned on and everybody washed away six days worth of filth. Water – precious, plentiful water accompanied our meal, which was followed by delivery of clean linens for the beds. And, as we suspected, Jack and I were summoned from our cell, escorted to the living quarters of Sgt. Bart Baker.

"You men tricked me."

"Maybe," Jack answered, "but it all worked out. You want us to trick you again?"

"I ain't queer. Don't think otherwise, or I'll tear you both a new asshole."

"We know you ain't queer," I jumped in. "Neither are we. But hell, there ain't any females around. What else are we supposed to do?"

He smiled and began to unbutton his shirt. "Nothing else to do. One thing's for sure, you two have had plenty of practice."

Silently, I enjoyed this hypocrisy. Sure, none of us are queer. Not much.

Jack and I partnered again to effectively queer up the sergeant. With Bart stripped naked and sprawled across his bed, we tongue bathed every inch of him, all the while making promises we knew we could keep.

"Thing is, Bart, those men worship us now," said Jack. "They'll work their ass off if we tell 'em to." He planted the tip of his tongue onto a nipple and began to delicately lick, as I spit out the toes in my mouth to further convince him.

"That's right. With plenty of food and water, these men will move like a bat out of hell for us, which means for you. I guarantee we'll finish on whatever day you like. You tell us and we'll get it done."

"God damn it," Bart raised his head to stare us down. "You both talk too much. I get it, ok? Be nice and we'll do anything. I heard you the first time. Now shut the fuck up. Do something useful with your mouths besides blathering non-stop."

That was the last word we heard from Bart or he from us.

He spread himself out into the shape of an X, while Jack and I worshiped him like he was a god. Just imagine it. Beneath our tongues lay a military man in his physical prime, body hard as concrete, but totally exposed and surrendered to our desires. There were long, drawn-out sessions of total desecration. Whatever I did, Jack duplicated it on a different Bart body part. No inch of this man's topside was left untouched. If Jack was licking our sergeant's manly feet and toes, I'd be on his thick fingers and hands. As Jack moved onto the meaty and furry calves, I'd tongue the triceps, biceps and arm pits. When Jack hit the muscular thighs, I assaulted the mighty chest and firm, high-topped nipples. As Jack buried Bart's powerfully throbbing and dripping cock into his sensuous mouth, my face and my lips slavishly praised Bart's rippling, hard belly.

Throughout this all-nighter, each assault was climaxed by bullets fired from the mighty gun of Sergeant Bart Baker – into our mouths, into our bowels, whichever happened to be covering him at the time. His muscular body glistened with our spit and was never allowed to dry. He was constantly licked and sucked to wetness by one of us, while the other brought forth manly explosions from that glorious cock. And from one night to the next, the three of us engaged in these all-nighters, until Jack and I delivered on our promise. Bart won the prize. Block A's pump station was completed 72 hours ahead of schedule, 48 hours before the second-place finish for the project assigned to Block D.

Of course, neither of us realized that the completion of our project would bring about an end to all we knew, including Bart, and worst of all, the relationship Jack and I had worked so hard to build. Our prison became a federal facility and we were transferred out. Jack and I ended up in different pens, never again to be paired together in the Texas state system of prisons.

It took me awhile to find out where Jack was housed, and once I did we sent letters back and forth for several years, until his to me stopped coming. Somewhere down the road I got word that he'd been stabbed and was dead, but I never could confirm it. I figured it was just some punk trying to get under my skin, which was impossible to do. I had been through it all, including several cell mates, some good, some insufferable, none Jack.

All told, mine was a 43-year sentence. They cut me loose and I headed back to New Mexico, back to the reservation, without ever knowing what it was Jack and I had helped to construct at our old facility. On the way out of Texas, I chose a bus route that would take me by the place and I strained my eyes when it came into view, but couldn't see much. The old prison grounds are surrounded by razor-wire-topped electrical fence set one mile in every direction away from the perimeter of that facility. Whatever the secret is will remain a secret to me.

I continued looking out the window as the bus passed by, while my mind reflected upon everything we did there – Jack, Max and Sergeant Bart Baker. Jack and I tamed him, that's for sure, and everybody involved came out better for it. I'm satisfied that, thanks to us, Bart learned how to finagle the best cock suckers around into handling that healthy slab of man meat between his legs. He certainly was a thing of beauty from head to toe and it was a pleasure to partake of him.

Crossing the state line into New Mexico was the end of it for me. I put both men out of my mind forever, knowing that such thoughts are useless to an old man returning to a society unknown to him – a society filled with people who could never understand why we did what we did.

DEATH BY TENOCHCAS

It would be a waste of time for me to try describing the emotions felt when a man knows that death is imminent – especially when that man knows well in advance every detail of how his end will come. My fellow soldiers and I had seen the rituals of human sacrifice performed time and again, but the victims killed were natives to this strange land. They were Indians, as we called them, and somehow the sight of their gruesome butchering did not seem nearly so tragic – not so much civilized humans, but more like animals led to slaughter.

This was different. Today's festival of blood was cause for great celebration amongst the Tenochcas – known now as Aztecs – because this was to be a glorious gift to the gods never before seen. The mysterious and powerful foreign invaders would offer their strong, beating hearts to the bloodthirsty Aztec deity, Huitzilopochtli.

We are Spaniards and we came here with Hernan Cortes to conquer this land and its people. Conquer we did. The history lesson is not important to me, but the events leading to our imprisonment are. Cortes was forced to leave us – 200 men, alone, to guard tens of thousands of Indians and their untold riches in gold. We had convinced them that we were nearly gods ourselves, but when Cortes was forced to return east and quell an uprising of natives there, the Aztecs slowly realized we were merely humans. Our trickery and deceit could not be successful forever and eventually the Aztecs overthrew their timid ruler, who had allowed our domination. We were made prisoners, shackled in chains.

The first few days were hell for me, as the agonizing screams of my fellow soldiers echoed one by one from atop the great pyramid. Next day – my turn, but I would be the last. They saved me for the grand highlight of their festival of blood, mainly so I could helplessly watch the agonizing torture and death of my beloved Tlaloc.

He was one of the young Aztec priests, a still learning disciple of the god Huehueteotl. Although he was dedicated to the priesthood, he had inexplicably become enraptured with me, and, since I was far from my homeland and feared no repercussions, I succumbed to his advances.

In the few days we had together before the uprising, his oral service upon me was like nothing I had ever known. The incredible praise on my manly phallus took me to incredible heights of ecstasy – so great in fact that I wanted to pleasure him in return. His coaxing told me what he desired and I gladly satisfied his every need.

I massaged and caressed his youthfully soft, bronzed skin, while gently maneuvering him onto his belly. As soon as my penis entered his anus, Tlaloc engulfed me with the muscles inside him. Soon, we were one complete being, as my twists and thrusts harmonized with his contractions and undulations to produce an orgasm for the ages.

Our pattern of togetherness became ritual. Each day he would come to me numerous times, seeking the satisfaction only I could give him. I anticipated his arrival with juices dripping, until he lovingly took them from me.

Once the uprising took place, I knew Tlaloc would be singled out as a collaborator. Worse yet, several of the jealous servant girls had become aware of what we were doing and related every detail to our captors.

Chained together with nine of my fellow soldiers, hidden away in a dark cell, I had not seen or heard anything about Tlaloc for several days. His fate was unknown to me, but I feared he would face what we all would face – a ritualistic death by torture. He, like us, would become a sacrificial victim atop the pyramid of the Great Temple.

When our time came, the ten of us were taken from the holding cell and led to the temple. There, we were unchained from each other, stripped naked and one by one led up countless steps to the pinnacled platform of their pyramid.

In the Aztec religion, only one type of sacrifice could appease the god Huitzilopochtli – living, beating hearts from human prisoners who had been defeated in battle.

Once the first of my fellow soldiers and his escorts reached the platform atop the pyramid, he was stretched chest up and spread eagled across the surface of a stone alter, his four limbs held by four priests. The high priest stood before his victim, chanted some sort of prayer and buried a glimmering, metal-bladed knife into the man's gut. He was cut open just below his rib cage. Through this opening, the priest reached in with bare hand to extract the soldier's heart from his chest cavity, and then held the still-beating organ high above his head for all to see. A great cheer echoed from the throngs below, and once he was satisfied that both his god and his subjects were pleased, the priest unceremoniously tossed the bloody lump into a pit of fire. Sacrifice made, the man's body was thrown down the stair case and taken away for disposal, while the spectators screamed with delight.

Nine had gone before me and now I stood alone awaiting my journey. As my escort led me to the first step, the high priest announced to the people the coming of a rare spectacle – two sacrifices together – one for Huitzilopochtli and one for Huehueteotl. A buzz reverberated from the mass of faithful crowding below the pyramid, because a human sacrifice to Huehueteotl was indeed a treasured and seldom seen event – a display of barbarity I would be forced to watch.

Completing our final step upwards, my escorts handed me over to the priests atop the temple. I stood on the platform near the alter and turned to see another entourage ascending the steps. Unrestrained, Tlaloc was surrounded by four priests who had been his teachers. All five were dressed in full ceremonial garb and Tlaloc seemed to be in some sort of semi hypnotic state.

Soon they reached the platform and stood before the high priest. Words were shouted at the shamed prisoner, as each article of priestly clothing was removed from him one by one. Tlaloc and I were now both naked and he turned his head to stare at me, but the eyes were glazed and he seemed not to recognize who I was or what was happening.

Suddenly, the four priests grabbed Tlaloc and hurled him into the pit of fire. Ten feet deep, the pit was an inverted pyramid, with four sides of stone angled to a degree which made it impossible to escape. Shrieks of agony echoed from the pit, as Tlaloc desperately tried to climb up the slick stone surface, but each time he would manage only to reach midway, before faltering to slide back down into the fire.

After what seemed countless minutes, his struggles and screams subsided a bit and his end became inevitable. No longer able to attempt escape from the pit, he pitifully moaned and uselessly dug his nails into the stone surface, while the fire relentlessly scorched his naked skin. Then, his body collapsed to lean still standing against the angled stone wall, while the flames lapped at his feet and legs. He became silent.

Death however, would not yet come for poor Tlaloc. I watched in horror, as two priests approached the pit with giant metal hooks, with which they proceeded to secure his limp body and pull it up from the fiery pit. In a ruthless display of sadistic cruelty, the four priests of the god Huehueteotl raised the roasted, but still living body above their heads and paraded it around the perimeter of the temple platform.

A wave of cheers enveloped the temple from the spectators below. Tlaloc gazed at me as his tortured form passed by and I made an attempt to rescue him, but my arms were quickly secured by the four priests assigned to me. I was forced to helplessly watch the macabre scene, while listening to the high priest shout incantations of mockery and revenge against the fallen Tlaloc.

The foreign shrieks pierced my ears, until I thought my head would explode. Then, the shouting stopped and Tlaloc was once again thrown into the pit of fire.

This horrific spectacle was repeated, as Tlaloc was allowed to cook for a short time before being fished out of the pit and again paraded about the platform. I lost count of the number of times they did this to him. After the fourth burning, boils and blisters covered his entire body and huge chunks of roasted flesh fell to the platform with each jolting step of parading priests. The once youthful and tantalizing form of Tlaloc had been transformed into a bloody nightmare of melted mush. He still looked at me as they passed by, but I no longer dared to return his hollowed gaze through eyelids blackened, boiled and partially missing.

It continued until he was brought out of the pit with practically no meat upon him. Only then did the high priest reach into the easily accessible chest cavity to remove Tlaloc's slowly beating heart. After some incantations, both the organ and lifeless body were cast into the pit of fire one final time. His unholy suffering had mercifully come to an end.

Now they turned to the final Spaniard. The priests led me to the stone alter and stretched my body across the top surface, while the high priest alerted their god that another victim would soon be his for the taking. Because I had desecrated and defiled one of their disciples, my penis was manually brought to erection, quickly severed and thrown into the fire.

Strangely, I was for the most part unaware of what was happening to me. My mind had been numbed since the first burning of Tlaloc and it seemed as though my nervous system had completely shut down. There was no response from me – no resistance and no pain.

This reverts to my original statement, regarding how it is impossible to describe one's emotions before inescapable death. I had none. I was well aware of what was happening to me, even at the moment of incision into my abdomen and the hand being thrust into my chest cavity, but I felt nothing. The day-long event, my witnessing of the drawn out deaths of nine Spaniards and one Aztec, had numbed me. My brain ceased to function, as did everything under its control. It did, however, absorb the signal sent from my eyes in those final two seconds, when my heart was ripped away from me. The impulse registered just long enough for me to glimpse the bloody thing being clutched in the elevated hand of the Aztec high priest.

Spiritually, I lingered awhile to witness them casting my body down the long ladder of stone steps. No honors for me, the once gallant Spanish warrior. All respect was stripped away – the penance paid for my defilement and corruption of their young disciple.

For a time afterwards I was hostile towards the Aztecs, but soon that hatred vanished. After all, we are the ones who disrupted their world. Their ritualistic human sacrifices may have seemed brutal and barbaric at the time, but who's to know what awaits us in the afterlife? Which gods are valid and what do those gods desire from humans living on the planet known as Earth? Should we fret over any of them, if any exist at all?

I know the answers, but I am not allowed to tell you. Let's just say that when it comes to cruelty, no human civilization is any better or any worse than any other. Tlaloc and I are no longer concerned with such things.

CHARLIE'S BOOK
Part One - Smoking is Allowed

"Private Charles Higdon, United States Army, 37337566 T42 43 0."

It is all he was trained to say.

Although he suffered, his body glowed with a powerfully masculine resilience, muscles tensing to withstand the torture and skin shining with layers of sweat. His interrogator, however, was not at all satisfied with the response.

"We have received intelligence that your General James Van Fleet will be inspecting the battlefield within days. You know this is true. You will tell us when and where."

No answer came from the naked prisoner, just a strain against the ropes securing his wrists and ankles. He was tied and suspended to a vertical, metal column, one of four that supported the ceiling of the concrete room. Two sets of aligned holes each had been drilled through this particular metal pole, one pair of which was approximately one foot from the ceiling and the other one foot from the floor. Through these holes, ropes had been threaded and this is how the interrogators had suspended their prisoner. His wrists were crossed and bound to the back side of the column, while his ankles were crossed and bound in the same manner below. With his arms stretched overhead, Private Higdon's chest, belly and thighs protruded towards his antagonists on the front side of the column.

"Your uncooperative actions will not help you. You will remain here until you talk."

Still silent, he dropped his head and relaxed, allowing the suspension to resume its purpose. His breathing was labored, but his strength could sustain him for several hours, and so, the Chinese would be forced to wait for their answers.

To speed the process, they intensified the pressure upon him. Bamboo sticks were brought from a side wall and two underlings began to wail upon the man's exposed skin. Every part of his front side was covered, as red welts started to form lines upon the flesh of his thighs, belly and chest. Each blow brought forth a slight whimper from the bound prisoner, but no words. Droplets of sweat flew in every direction, as the lead interrogator stood back, watched and waited for the soldier to cry out – to beg for release or an end to the beatings. Hearing none of this, the henchman decided to let the man rest. He knew that the lingering effects of these bamboo whippings would, in reality, allow his prisoner no rest.

"Enough," he barked, and all beatings stopped. "We will let him think on it for awhile..."

It is at this point that I also paused to rest. These descriptions are my words, derived from the soldier's words, and the Chinese interrogator's quotations are exactly as the soldier remembered them.

I closed the diary from which I had gleaned those words in an attempt to distance myself from the horrific scene I was forced to type – my summary of his hastily written hand. The goal? To transform his diary into a book. A book which was to be a vivid retelling of wartime experiences – more specifically, about the exploits of my pal, Charlie.

Even though Charlie and I were employed at the same place, our meeting probably never would have occurred without changes in company smoking regulations. We both worked for the major daily newspaper in town, but in vastly different departments. While I was a desk sitting pencil pusher in one building, Charlie worked in the hot, dirty confines of another building that housed the printing presses.

Grease, ink, oil and many other working-man substances usually blotched his coveralls and lined the undersides of his fingernails, and while some might find this offensive, I thought it only enhanced his already masculine presence, which featured a barreled chest and just the right amount of brown hairs on meaty forearms.

The muckety-mucks who ran the newspaper had decided that smoking would no longer be allowed inside the buildings, so those of us who did took our breaks congregated in the little plaza built outside the main entrance and in between our three buildings. The first time I saw him come out the door, my eyes brightened.

Whether or not he initially noticed me is unclear, but as fate would have it his disposable lighter would not fire up, clearly out of fluid. My cigarette was already lit and as he searched every pocket for matches, I waved my Zippo at him, so he swaggered down the three stairs to join me.

"Dried up on you, did it?" I handed him my lighter.

He seemed a bit skeptical, because the desk jockeys normally didn't socialize much with the laborers, but I wasn't that way. In my storied list of career changes, I had been both blue collar and white collar, so I felt comfortable with just about anybody who wasn't a jerk. He picked up on this right away.

Flipping open the cover, he shook his head, "Yeah, I knew it was almost empty, but figured it would be ok inside. Forgot that today was no more inside."

As he fired up the smoke, I noticed the first finger of his right hand was cut off at the last joint. He handed the lighter back to me and thanked me.

After returning it to my white dress shirt pocket, I proceeded to bitch. "It's going to be great fun out here when winter comes."

"Well, we smokers are just criminals, ya know? They don't give a damn 'bout us."

"Nope, we worker drones are just their little peons."

"That's exactly right. They pee on us all the time."

This gave me good reason to smile, not that I found it outrageously funny, but it did set the tone for a care-free conversation. Plus, like I said, he was right up my alley when it comes to man forms, so I proceeded without caution. "Bet you work with the press machines. Nobody gets dirty like you guys. Is that where you lost part of your finger?"

"No, that was Korea."

"As in Korean War?"

"Yep. 23rd Infantry Regiment, Second Infantry Division. First ground forces deployed directly from the United States to engage the enemy."

"Thank you."

He glared at me for a few seconds, not sure whether I was showing respect or just trying to be a smart-ass. "For what?"

"For going through that hell... for me... for all of us."

I think he was genuinely touched by this and although part of my motives were sinister, in reality I meant it – especially for Korean War veterans. Guys returning from World War II were instant heroes; guys from Viet Nam were first scorned, then pitied, then finally given the tributes they deserved; but Korean War vets were and still are mostly ignored.

He held out his right hand, "I'm Charlie Higdon."

"John Garrison. I process obituaries."

We shook hands, which was followed by a pleasurable silence, as we inspected one another with mutual admiration and took the last drags from our cigarettes.

"I guess after all these years, I finally know why I ended up in that god-forsaken country," he smirked, daring me to ask him.

"Oh, yeah? What?"

"To prepare me for standing out here in the freezing cold, just for the privilege of having a smoke."

"Well, maybe you can train me on how to deal with it. At least now I won't go through half a pack during the day. These new rules will save me lots of money."

"Hey, pal, I really do appreciate what you said. I didn't mean to brush it off like it doesn't matter," he grinned and once again offered his hand as a way to confirm his sincerity. "Hope to see you again."

"Hope so, too," I replied, relishing the firm grip of his thick, working-man fingers. "My next break is around 12:30, so if you need a light, look me up. By the way, Charlie, I've always felt gratitude towards veterans. I'll thank them any way I can."

My eyes locked onto his crotch as I continued, "I was born a few years after you were over there, so I never had to serve. By the time I came of age, we had pulled out of Viet Nam. Maybe I feel guilty because I never had to serve, but whatever, that's just the way it is."

He dropped his cigarette to the ground and stepped on it with his steel toed work shoe, while grabbing his hidden peter and giving it an adjustment. "Think I'll be out here around 12:30 myself."

"Ok, see you."

The 12:30 conversation set everything up and I wasted no time in confirming it.

"So, quitting time's 4:30 for me. How about you, Charlie?"

"Same."

"Great. Meet me out here and I'll give you my special veteran's treatment." Of course, my eyes were transfixed on his groin, as I forced him to respond. "That is, if you're up for it."

With a mischievous grin, he agreed to my suggestion. "I won't be hard to find."

We met in the same plaza and headed for my car, which I figured would give us the necessary privacy.

"I know a spot over by the Montgomery grain elevators, Charlie. Nobody's ever around."

"Nah, that ain't no good. Where do ya live?"

This was moving along better than expected. "Got an apartment at Cypress Gardens. Want me to head over there?"

"Sure, John, if it's available."

"It's all mine... just me and myself."

"Hit it."

Charlie looked even better without the dark grey coveralls. The printing press guys had shower stalls and lockers for clean up before going home and now he wore blue jeans and a plaid, button up shirt with the top three buttons open, which exposed a plentiful supply of chest hair.

My first inclination was to get a hand on his bulge and make sure he was ready when we got to where we were going, but for some reason I stopped myself. Maybe I didn't want to know what was in there until I could actually see it, but truthfully I think it was because I felt an unexplainable pride being near him and hoped he felt the same about me.

Playing with his pecker while trying to drive would perhaps demean our new friendship. I hardly knew the guy, but somehow I sensed that he needed for me to be more than just a cock sucker to him. Because of this, I decided to remain patient and allow him to display himself when he felt comfortable doing so.

We rode up the elevator to the eighth floor in silence, then entered my apartment.

"Want something to drink, Charlie... beer, soda, water, liquor?"

"I like bourbon straight." He lit a cigarette.

"Ice?"

"Three cubes."

He followed me to the kitchen and I made the same drink for both of us. "How long have you been at the Post, Charlie?"

"Twenty-nine years. Thirty in August."

"Wow. You gonna retire soon?"

"Doubt if I will. I'm only 55. Got nothing else to do."

I handed him his drink. He took a sip and nodded his approval, then we journeyed to the living room to sit on the couch.

"Hell, you could retire and start a second career."

"Nah, when my workin' days are over, they're over for good. I'm happy where I am for now."

"I guess that makes sense. You can kick back and spend time with the grand kids. Do whatever you want when you want. That's the reward for working your ass off day after day."

"Got no grand kids, John."

There was a pause of silence and his eyes drifted past me, then he swallowed his remaining liquor and handed the glass to me. "Let's go. I'm ready."

Following me to the bedroom, Charlie wasted no time. He stripped naked and plopped onto the bed almost as quickly as I could get the covers peeled back. He stacked the pillows and laid his head in the middle of them, tucking one hand behind the head and the other clutching his peter.

"Let me get it revved up for ya."

He pumped it with his fist and it began to swell, then he released it and locked both hands behind his head, stretched out chest up and was ready to go.

After kicking off my shoes, I climbed to kneel between his thighs, leaned down and lifted his cock into my mouth. With moist lips locked onto the shaft, I began to stroke up and down, licking and scraping with my tongue. The organ ballooned to full strength and I shifted into my serious gear.

It didn't take me long to find his hot spot – that little triangle of sensitive skin underneath the crown. I knew this because Charlie's body jolted when I touched it and he interrupted the silence, "God damn, John. I think I've found me a pro - fessional."

He closed his eyes, fully aware that he was in for a treat, and as I worshiped him with all the techniques years of experience had brought to me, Charlie drifted deeper and deeper into whatever fantasy was running through his mind. This gave me a good chance to scrutinize what lay beneath me and what I saw pleased me no end. Thick, stocky, masculine beauty, highlighted with handsome swirls of golden brown body hair – just enough to label him a man, not a gorilla. Charlie exposed was everything I had hoped to see.

He never said a word or made a sound – even the breathing seemed relaxed and easy, as he thoroughly enjoyed all that my lips and tongue had to offer. I glanced down to inspect his legs, while methodically and slowly stroking with oral precision, but before I could get a good look, his body tensed up. The silence was shattered, as

Charlie belted out a rather unusual orgasmic expression, "Ughhh, yankee ma, you bastards!"

With a mighty exhale of air, he contracted and I waited. Charlie's orgasm had come, but the product was a mere trickle. He just laid there all tensed up with eyes closed and an anguished expression on his face, but made no verbal or guttural sounds. Then, the body slowly relaxed and contractions subsided, so I orally squeezed from the base of his cock to the head, forcing out anything that I might have missed during his convulsions.

After removing his fading peter from my mouth, I laid it onto his belly and raised up to look at him. He remained motionless with eyes closed, but now a slight smile consumed his face, as he slowly returned to reality and rejoined me in my bedroom. "My god, Johnnie. You are something else."

"Yeah, well, I had a good project to work on."

"Come here."

He opened his eyes and motioned for me to lay beside him, so I crawled up and used his arm pit for a pillow, then rubbed his chest with my right hand.

"It's been a long time, John. I needed that."

I didn't respond, but instead enjoyed the comfort of our comedown. He seemed completely at ease in my presence, which was reassuring for me. Sometimes men act like they did something wrong after getting a queer blow job and as a result, they lash out at the queer who did it. But not this guy. He was totally confident in who and what he was and I think quite pleased with himself – pleased with his performance and pleased with his discovery of me. Apparently, my service was more than satisfactory, but I wondered if he knew that his well was nearly dry. Hell, he had to know, but obviously didn't care what I thought about it.

"Well, Johnnie, I think I'll ask you for another shot of that whiskey, then you better take me back to my car."

He told me when to stop pouring, then slammed back two more fingers of alcohol. After he dressed and relieved himself in my toilet, we headed down in the elevator.

On the drive back, Charlie asked me a serious question. "Hey, John, did you mean what you said about veterans or was it just a ploy to get my dick?"

"No, I meant every word of it. Tell you something else, too. As far as Korea goes, I think you guys got the shaft big time. I've read how when you first came home, people were afraid you fellows had turned Communist, especially the P.O.W.'s."

I turned to look at him, but he was staring down to the floorboard and seemingly lost in thought. It dawned on me that perhaps he had been one of those prisoners of war. Figuring I had touched a nerve, I made sure he knew exactly what I was trying to say.

"I wasn't born yet, Charlie, but I've read and thought about it. Harry Truman was right. Stop Communist aggression and eventually the Soviet Union will collapse on itself. We're seeing the beginnings of it now. Their economy is in ruins and the people are rejecting the system. You guys were the first ground forces committed to that philosophy. It started in Korea, but nobody in this country gives a shit – if they know about it at all. I hear these clowns saying Ronald Reagan did it and it pisses me off, because he had nothing to do with it. The Truman Doctrine worked, Charlie, and you were part of it. That's why I thanked you."

He remained silently staring downward, so I never looked at him again until I parked next to his car and waited for him to exit. Only then did he turn to face me, "John, I need to see you again."

"I think that's a good idea. When?"

"Tomorrow. Same routine."

"Ok, I'll see you, same time and place."

The pattern was established. For the next three days, Charlie would ride with me, get his dick sucked and let me take him back to his car. Each day, he would ask me to remove part of my wardrobe. First the shirt; next day the pants and socks; then finally, all the way naked.

Of course, it was impossible for me to keep my hands off of him, but I did explore with delicate care, beginning with day number two on the tops of his thighs. I felt an initial tensing of his muscles, but within seconds they relaxed and he said nothing, so I slid my hands over his knee caps and moved towards his hairy shins. Satisfied with that, I retraced my route, delicately bringing both hands to his inner thighs. My fingers lightly touched his testicles, at which time Charlie broke his silence.

"Oh, god no... not that."

His protest was not voiced in anger, nor was it expressed with kindness. His tone was more of a pleading for me to not touch him there, a begging, almost as though my contact with his nuts had pained him. Nothing could be further from the truth, but considering that this brief, one-second encounter had caused his penis to lose nearly one half its strength, I clamped both my hands onto my knees and left them there. From that point on, my service was strictly oral.

The next day, I allowed my hands to venture in the other direction, first on his belly, then his stomach and then his chest. Charlie's response was much more satisfying. A slight moan of pleasure seeped from his lips and I even sensed him flattening his middle section just a bit, while raising his chest just a bit, as he enjoyed my hand-warmed massaging and wet-tongued stroking.

One tiny spurt per day, that's what Charlie was good for and after each event I was invited to lay with my head on his chest. Other than my progressive states of undress, nothing varied, including the strange utterance he exhaled when orgasm came.

Normally, I would never allow such a mystery to keep me stumped, but with Charlie I found myself becoming subservient. For the first time in my life, I respected a man for something other than his penis and I allowed him to take us wherever he wanted to go. I quit asking questions and instead let him lead me with his actions, until we found ourselves on my bed and both of us fully stripped.

"Sorry, I think I got dribble on your leg, Charlie. My pecker drips syrup like a faucet."

"It's ok."

I laid my head on his chest and massaged him with my hand, while we both relaxed and caught our breath. Then, without warning, Charlie raised up and cast me off of him. He grabbed my shoulders and positioned me where he had just been, then planted kisses in a line starting at my chest, down to the stomach and onto the head of my still throbbing peter.

"Let me stop that leak," he warned, before taking my cock into his lips.

From that moment forward, I belonged to him.

Charlie's service was not highly-recommended from a technical aspect, but the emotions triggered by this unexpected gift made his mouth feel like utopia to me.

I glanced down to see the top of his head twisting and turning, then photographed the sight and closed my eyes. Knowing he felt this way about me brought orgasm quickly and soon we were again laying together, but this time in a side to side embrace. I buried my face into his chest, while wrapping my arm tightly around and pressing into his back. "Thank you, Charlie."

He kissed the top of my head and we stayed like this for not long enough.

"John, tomorrow's Friday and I need you to come to my house. Will you do it?"

This caused me to remove my face from him. "For dinner or what?"

"I need you to spend the weekend with me. Will you do it?"

I noticed how he said 'need' and not 'want'. More than this, I was a little confused as to what we would be doing at his house.

"I guess I can, but aren't you married? You wear a ring."

"No, John, I'm a widower. I live alone. Will you do it?"

How could I reject him? He looked at me with a nearly desperate longing, as though nobody had cared for him in the past 20 years.

"Sure, Charlie, I'll come."

He showed no emotion from my answer, but continued with a stern expression on his face – one of urgency. "Wait in your car like always. I'll meet you there and you can follow me."

"Ok. That'll work. Want me to stay both nights?"

"Yes."

Once we were in my car and headed back to his, there was no conversation whatsoever. It was the first time this had happened to us. The air was thick and tense, with me not willing to ask for more details and him not offering. Hell, I couldn't even think of any mundane subjects for us to cover, like work related, sports or current news events, so we both allowed this drive to become uncomfortable. But when I parked next to his car, Charlie looked around the empty parking lot, then leaned over to peck my cheek with a kiss. "See you tomorrow."

All was right again, although I didn't sleep much that night. My head buzzed with curiosity. Wherever this was headed had to be uncharted territory for me, because normally, I could get a man off and go about my business as though nothing much had happened. Not so with this man. Charlie was looking for a little more than that. I couldn't begin to guess what he needed from me, but I sensed it went well beyond more blow jobs, and I anticipated that the coming weekend might be one I would never forget.

Part Two - The Relaxin' Room

After a few minutes, the bamboo sticks again were laid to his helpless body. He tried desperately to avoid the blows, but there was nowhere to go. Bound and suspended to the round, metal pole running the length of his back, Private Higdon abandoned his resistance, instead staring blankly forward to accept one after another of the stinging, skin-breaking, bamboo whips to his naked body.

"Now will you talk?"

He gasped for air. Tiny droplets of blood trickled from countless red lines upon his skin. He dropped his chin to his chest and closed his eyes in an attempt to deal with his exhaustion – with his agonizing pain.

"Rinse him off." Cold water from two buckets was thrown at him, followed by another bucket-full poured over his head to wash away the sweat and blood. Then, the three Chinese left the room. Charles Higdon was abandoned to his suspended agony. Thirst further tormented him, while his skin burned and throbbed from the ruthless bamboo beatings. Minutes passed like hours, as he drifted into light sleep, only to be awakened by unholy pain. He gazed down his expanded chest to count each red line as a way to keep his mind focused on the here and now. No thoughts of home could be entertained – no thoughts of his Army buddies or anything else outside this hideous room.

Fear and anger raged through him. His anger was focused on Wo Chin, the interrogator. This man was dressed in civilian, not military clothing and this is what triggered the prisoner's fear. No recognized Geneva Convention doctrines or codes of conduct would apply, not for this soldier. He realized the possibility existed that he could be tortured until either he talked or he died. No one outside this room would know the difference. Charles Higdon was just another Army regular who had gone missing...

Again I was forced to halt my typing. Putting together this first draft to tell the nightmare of Charlie's plight saddened me, but since I knew the end of the story, I could reflect on our first weekend together to temporarily ease my mind.

With my overnight bag resting on the back seat of my car, I waited for Charlie to arrive. He pulled up with his driver's door next to mine.

"All set?"

"Yep."

"Staying two nights?"

"Yep."

"Here we go."

And with that we drove to the suburbs. His was a rather ordinary house – split level, part brick, part wood frame, two car garage attached on the right, manageably small yard in front. I guessed it to be a house built in the 1960's and as I watched Charlie get out and open both garage doors, I imagined him playing in the yard with his children way back when he was a young man himself. Then I thought about the possibility that he and his wife never got around to starting a family, but I figured all would be explained soon enough.

He motioned me into the far end of the garage, then hopped into his car to ease it in the near side. I got out to help him close the doors.

"Ever think about getting automatic doors, Charlie?"

"Yeah, but for just one person, why bother?"

Grabbing my bag, I followed him into the house, where the first room seen was the kitchen. Something smelled heavenly and I wanted to linger here, but Charlie led me past that room into the dining room, then down a hallway. The interior of the house looked clean and smelled fresh. He opened the door to show me his bedroom and a queen sized bed.

"Put your bag in here. We'll settle in later."

He waited for me and I did as asked, then joined him in the hallway as he closed the door behind me.

"You want a drink?"

"Sure. Same as at my place if you got it."

Two bourbons on the rocks were poured in the kitchen and Charlie led me up two steps to a room above the garage.

"This is my relaxin' room."

Here was a comfy leather sofa and matching chair with ottoman, plus a corduroy recliner, the three of which formed a semicircle. Also, there was a television, stereo, end tables, coffee table, two windows looking over the driveway and various pictures on the walls. It was a cheerful and inviting room, except that the blinds were drawn and it was rather dark. Charlie turned on a lamp to brighten things up. "Have a seat."

I sank down into the sofa, while he took the recliner angled to the right of me. We sat quietly and rested for awhile, slowly sipping our whiskey and of course, puffing on our cigarettes. Soon, the silence started to annoy me.

"This sofa's great. I could almost fall asleep."

"Yeah, that's what I do every time I sit or lay down on the damn thing. Can't help it."

Another uncomfortable quiet settled in and I wondered what he had planned. It seemed as though whatever was on his mind couldn't make it to his tongue, so I tried to guide him along.

"So, this must be where you spend most of your time."

He stood and walked to a wall, lifting one of the picture frames off of its hook. "This was our kid's bedroom. Lookee here."

I took the black and white photo from him to see four people – Charlie with his buzz cut hair, but much younger face and thinner body; a pretty lady wearing a pair of those "Cat Woman" shaped eyeglasses; a girl that looked to be about 10 years old and a boy around five. They were dressed as though going to church and standing between two single beds, clearly in the very room where I now sat.

"This was taken in 1962, not long after we bought this house."

"Sure are cute children, Charlie... just like their mom and dad."

"Yeah, they were."

He sat on the sofa next to me and pointed at the photo. "That's Jane. We called her Janie. She was eleven and Michael – I called him Mike, he was five. Janie's mine and Mike we adopted in '58."

"And your wife?"

He took the frame from me and gazed down at it. "That's Marsha. We were married in 1950 right after we graduated from high school. Janie was born while I was overseas."

I said nothing and waited for more, but after staring at the photo for what seemed countless seconds, Charlie stood up and returned it to the wall. "Well, I'm hungry. There's a brisket been cooking all day in the oven. You ready?"

"Sure, Charlie. Whenever you are."

I suspect the beef came from a butcher shop, because no grocery store meat could melt in a person's mouth the way Charlie's brisket melted in mine. Our dinner was consumed in the dining room. The conversation was pleasant and mostly non personal, but he did ask me if I had ever thought about doing the marriage and family thing.

"Well, I almost did. My girlfriend got pregnant during our senior year of high school."

"Ah-hah, so you do know what pussy feels like."

"Oh, sure, but it is a fading memory."

"What happened to the kid? Aborted?"

"No, she wanted to have it, but our parents took charge of the situation. Once they got us to confess that we really didn't love each other and didn't want to get married, they got lawyers to set everything up like I would pay child support until the kid turned 18."

"Did you ever know the child?"

"No. Saw her in the delivery room and never again. Mutual agreement."

"How old is she now?"

I swallowed the last of my meal and figured it up. "Born in 1974, so 13 years. Five more and I get to keep all of my money. They don't need it. She and her mom and dad live near Chicago. He's some kind of hot shot, grain broker at the Board of Trade, so I'm sure she's had a privileged life."

"What did you name her?"

"Her mother named her Kristen."

"That's pretty." Charlie picked up the empty plates. "You regret it?"

"No. I try not to think about it too much – you know, about how different my life could've been."

We cleared the table and took everything into the kitchen, then I helped him load the dishwasher.

"Yeah, John, things happen that take us in different directions. Most times we don't know why until we get there."

"Usually ends up for the best, though, even if we can't see it at the time."

Charlie hesitated, reflecting before answering. "Well, I guess that's true some of the time... don't know about usually."

"Thanks for dinner. You're a good cook."

"I suppose you'd like to know how I came to be a widower, huh?"

"I'm not going to pry, Charlie. It's up to you."

"C'mon, let's get comfortable and I'll tell you. You want another drink?"

With a glass of bourbon in hand, I returned to the sofa, while Charlie took another picture from the wall. He sat in his recliner and handed the frame to me.

"That's my Buick and her Studebaker. Taken the same year as the other picture."

A big four door Buick with the chrome teeth in front was coupled in the driveway of 25 years ago by a Studebaker coupe.

"When I got back from overseas, I kicked around a few meaningless jobs before hooking up at the newspaper in 1957. In 1962, they made me shift foreman. We had just bought this house, so the timing couldn't have been better."

I laid the frame onto my lap and looked at Charlie, as he continued.

"Now, it was my function to drop Janie off at school and Mike at daycare. Marsha had a part time job in a dress shop over by where we used to live, so she picked them up in the afternoons. The morning I started my new foreman job, I got a call from a fellow up the street telling me his car wouldn't start and he needed a ride to work. Since I wouldn't have time to take both him and the kids, I had to make a decision, because I sure as hell wasn't gonna be late for work on this day."

He stopped and turned a little to his left, so he could look me in the eye. "I chose my neighbor and asked Marsha to take the kids to school. You know the Rockton overpass?"

"Sure, goes over 69 Highway."

"Well, in those days 69 Highway was a narrow two-lane. The overpass was tight underneath. A big old dump truck was heading south and hit the concrete side of that thing, then bounced into the northbound lane, where the white Studebaker on your lap just happened to be at the time."

Here he stopped and I sat in stunned silence. Charlie looked at me unfazed, with eyes stern and cold, almost daring me to ask the obvious. "You lost all three?"

"Right then and there."

My eyes started to water, but I fought it. I knew he didn't need that, so I tried to speak, but couldn't think of what to say. After 25 years, it seemed meaningless to tell him how awful it was or how sorry I was or any other useless, apologetic speeches. After all, it wasn't my fault. What I felt was gratitude for being made to feel closer to him, so without thinking I blurted it out.

"Thanks for sharing it with me, Charlie."

The hard expression on his face quickly softened and a slight smile appeared, "You are a rarity, John, you truly are. How 'bout another drink?"

I held up my glass and watched him leave the room. Staring at the picture, I tried to imagine what that poor car must have looked like after the event. What I tried to avoid was what the people inside must have looked like, and mercifully, Charlie returned with two more bourbons on ice. He sat on the sofa next to me and raised his glass to meet mine with a clank.

After a couple of swallows, Charlie resumed the story.

"Here's the thing. I did the neighborly thing and chose my supposed friend over my wife and children. You know what that son of a bitch did?"

"What."

"Dumped me – abandoned me. In fact, after my family was killed, this whole god damned neighborhood acted like it was my fault or something."

"How the hell could they figure that?"

"Think about it, John. Put yourself back to that time. It was before the women's lib movement. This was still a little bedroom community outside the city and it was highly unfashionable for a man to make his wife work. Her function was to stay at home, be a mother and housekeeper."

I laughed with an angry sarcasm. "That's stupid. If she'd have been a homemaker she'd be taking the kids every morning, so she would have been under that bridge anyway."

"Exactly. But in their hypocritical way of thinking, I was the one who put her in that situation. I was the one who decided my neighbor was more important than my family. It was my fault, so I was scorned by everybody out here, whether they knew me or not."

He brought the tumbler to his lips and downed two healthy gulps of whiskey, then continued. "You should have heard their phony boo hoo's at the funeral. Hell, we hadn't lived here long enough for them to be that upset about it. They didn't know us. They were just there to put on some drama. I could see it and feel it, John. Made me wanna puke.

Of course, the irony is that with my promotion, Marsha was gonna quit her job at that dress shop. We had planned for her to be that stay at home mom, but nobody knew that yet besides us."

I was reluctant to speak. Despite the gory consequences of his story, I was thankful that Charlie was comfortable enough with me to release these frustrations in my presence, and I did not want to interrupt his unraveling. I felt honored to be his chosen audience. Somehow, I wanted to absorb some of his pain, to alleviate his sadness and anger. He was sharing himself with me and my immediate desire was to accept everything he wanted to give, plus everything he would let me take. For now, I wanted to feel him and to smell him, so I scooted closer and tilted my head against his shoulder. Sensing my need, Charlie raised his arm and allowed me to use his right pectoral as a pillow.

Inexplicably, Charlie did not continue. I listened to him breathe. I heard his heart beat at an accelerated rate. I saw his leg wiggling back and forth – a nervous, antagonized twitch. And I decided to coax him along.

"So, why did you stay here, Charlie?"

"To frost 'em, Johnnie boy."

"Oh, I get it. Hang around and make everybody nervous."

"Sure, it's great comedy. They expected me to sell this house and run away, but I didn't. I stayed right here and made it my home, with my touch. Year after year, I'd entertain myself when they'd move away or better yet... die. Anytime I'd see a moving van, I'd be sure to stop by and tell 'em I'd sure miss 'em, even though they hadn't seen or spoken to me in years. You should've seen the looks on their faces. They didn't know what the hell to say."

I lifted my right hand for a sip of whiskey, then stretched my arm to set the tumbler on the end table. This is so my right hand could fiddle with the buttons on his shirt. "Are any of those people still around?"

"Don't know of any. Don't care anymore. I got bored with taunting them. It's a great lesson in knowing who your friends are, though. I haven't had very many since, so when I feel comfortable with someone it's a pretty big deal."

With two buttons undone by me, coupled with the three he never fastened, I now had easy access to his chest and belly. My right hand began to massage. Somehow, I found his belly button and lightly fingered the outer rim, moving in circles progressively deeper into the hole, which brought a favorable reaction.

"I'll bet you're sick of this room. How 'bout I show you my bedroom."

"Thought you'd never ask."

In the darkness, my tongue and lips savored every inch of him from the neck to his toes, with the exception of that aforementioned, do-not-touch area. Charlie lay quietly and basked in my unwavering devotion to him. I got what I wanted – his smell, his taste, the texture of his skin and nose-tickling body hairs, until my worship of him culminated in the inevitable. I found his penis and slavishly praised it. Those words – again I heard that mysterious phrase of words, while sampling a mere trace of semen.

We slept off and on like husband and wife, with him on his back and me on his chest. And to further consecrate the roles we would play, Charlie woke me sometime in the still darkness with a whispered request.

"Johnnie, can I get inside you?"

I did not bother to tell him that no one had been there since I first reconciled my homosexuality, nor did I bother to tell him that I did not like it and had never allowed it again. I belonged to this man. Anything he asked of me would be granted, and while his oral service on me had been a pleasant surprise, his anal intercourse was a new found heaven.

The gentle at first, then dominantly powerful progression brought stimulation to me I never knew could exist, and the pain of my long ago experience vanished, as did my memory of it. Charlie was different. Charlie was inside me to please me – to be the best man he could possibly be for me, and because he was such a soul, a man just as beautiful on the inside as on the out, I, in turn, responded for him. I quickly learned to accept and worship his penis with my innards, soon matching the expertise with which I had worshiped him when using my lips, roof of mouth and tongue.

We were on the fast track. Two loners had stumbled across one another to find their lives changing in ways unpredictable and unavoidable. We did not have the time or desire to think about where we were going. After his exit from me and the cleanup, we both slept peacefully naked in each other's arms.

Part Three - The Book

When Wo Chin and his henchmen finally returned, Higdon was nearly unconscious. The stifling heat and stagnant air in the concrete room had caused sweat to again drench him, while lack of water nearly drove him mad with thirst.

"I am growing impatient. Will you talk? Tell us about the General."

Higdon opened his eyes to glare at the tormentor, flexed his chest in defiance and said nothing.

"Very well, prepare him.

Four men now assisted the interrogator and the prisoner was released from his pole. Draped over a Chinese shoulder, his limp body was carried to a 12 feet long by five feet wide wooden table. There, he was laid face up and spread-eagle. At four corners, four holes had been drilled and ropes threaded through each hole. One end of each was tied to the prisoner's wrists and ankles, while the other ends ran to hand cranks mounted underneath the table surface.

Once secured, Higdon's limbs were stretched taut in four opposing directions, as the hand cranks were turned and locked into position to tighten the ropes. Now, Wo Chin hovered above his victim's anguished face.

"Soon you will tell me all I need to know."

Higdon inspected his restraints. He feebly pulled against the ropes, causing his chest to expand and muscles to flex, but he knew escape was impossible. Naked, helpless and alone, he was consumed by this degrading vulnerability. He mentally prepared himself for whatever agony would soon come.

"This is your last chance. Talk now."

He continued his struggle, shuddering to see four small alligator clamps tauntingly waved before his face. He felt the tiny teeth pinch his skin in four places, one on each of his nipples, and two more on the flesh of his testicles. Wires were attached to each clamp, then Private Higdon heard squeaking wheels, as Wo Chin pushed a cart near the head end of the table within his prisoner's view. Atop the cart was a generator. Wo Chin attached the wires to its metal posts.

The soldier closed his eyes and mentally prepared for what he knew would come, if such a thing is possible.

The switch was thrown and a devastating jolt racked his body. Immediately, his back arched and every muscle tensed to capacity. His toes curled, fists and teeth clenched, while a deep, guttural groan of agony rumbled from the depths of his chest. He summoned every ounce of strength to endure this unholy electro torture...

Somehow, I could almost feel the voltage raging through me as it had him. I knew this beautiful man – I had touched him, grown close to him, given him pleasure, and the thought of what he had endured all those years ago was nearly too much for me. But his story had to be told. It was no longer a desire, but an obsession.

The next morning was Saturday and Charlie thoughtfully woke me by using his mouth on my penis. He had been taking mental notes, remembering the techniques I had used on him and using them with authority on me. Together, we made a hefty breakfast of eggs, toast, bacon, fruit and coffee, which was a treat for me, but routine for him.

"Every morning starts like this for me. Otherwise, I'm no good. Your belly is like your feet, John. If those parts aren't happy, then none of the rest of you is either."

A man in the morning in the kitchen in his underwear is a sight to see, and I let him know about it.

"Well, Charlie, your belly and your feet are two of my favorite parts, so for God's sake take good care of them." This was accompanied by a from-behind, double-handed rub to his hairy, hard-muscled slab of middle section.

"Come on, now," he laughed. "How can I take care of myself if I'm constantly in bed with you? That's where we're headed, if you don't calm down."

"Ok, Charlie, I'll be good. Let's eat."

Afterwards, he showered and I cleaned up our mess. I was reading the newspaper on that leather sofa when Charlie entered dressed and refreshed.

"John, I've gotta run a few errands. I need you to read this while I'm gone."

He handed me a brown, leather-bound booklet, which appeared to be well-worn. The size was that of a handbook.

"When I got back from overseas, my court appointed attorney

advised me to write these things down. It didn't do me any good, because I still spent two years in Leavenworth, but I need you to read it anyway."

As I clutched the nondescript book in my hand to inspect the weathered and nameless cover, the garage door opened below me and engine started. Inlaid to the center of the book cover was a small American flag. The red, white and blue colors had dulled with time and wear, but the beauty of it stirred emotions nonetheless. Then, the door closed and motor sound faded from driveway to street to oblivion. I opened the book.

Events as I Remember Them.
Pvt. Charles Higdon, United States Army, 37337566 T42 43 0
I was taken September 16, 1951 near Yangimal, Korea.
Thus began my descent into Charlie's hell.

Tank Books

Part Four - Eradication

He was captured by North Koreans, but turned over to Chinese. They wanted to know the schedule for General James Van Fleet, second in command for United Nations ground forces.

Charlie was tortured for an unknown number of hours, until he gave them the name of a town – not 'yankee ma' as I thought I had heard him say so often, but Yangimal, a village near the battle of Heartbreak Ridge. Charlie was forced to give the time of the General's arrival in this area and once he did, they turned him back over to the Koreans.

His physical torture ended, but psychological torture continued for 19 months. He was kept in isolation, confined to a small concrete cell with no fixtures and no regulation of temperatures. He suffered through bitter cold in winter and ungodly heat in summer. He was made to go days at a time without food. The sanitary conditions were abhorrent and every day they would badger him with speeches on the virtues of Communism. They wanted him to sign statements denouncing the United States and the United Nations. They wanted him to sign statements that the U.S. military had used poison gases and massacred civilians for sport. He signed nothing.

Of course, he didn't know the date when he was released, but was told by the Army it was April 24, 1953. Unlike most prisoners, who were participants of prearranged P.O.W. exchanges, Charlie's release was more of an abandonment. He described how he was taken by vehicle with hands tied behind his back and dumped on a trail in a barren, mountainous area. He watched them drive away, then trudged eastward until he came across an encampment of the Eighth Army. His body weight had dropped to 86 pounds.

This summation does not begin to address the gruesome details of Charlie's ordeal, written by his own hand. Several times I was forced to lay the book aside, distancing myself from those images before I could continue.

But I did finish it, then closed the book and laid it beside me on the sofa. This chapter of the story had ended. The rest would have to come from him, so I closed my eyes and waited... and waited. Whatever these errands were, Charlie had been gone for nearly two hours.

When he did return I was in the shower. After stopping in the kitchen to pour my last cup of coffee, I found him in his recliner and the book on the sofa where I had left it.

"Did you read all of it?"

"Every word. Where'd you go?"

"Hardware store. There's some stuff you can help me unload later."

I took my seat beside the book. "It was not easy to read this, Charlie."

"Wasn't easy to write it either. Thing is, it was just plain stupid how I came to be captured."

"How so?"

"Buddy of mine from Waterloo, Iowa named Bill Harvey talked me into slipping into that village one night. That was Yangimal. Had a Korean girl he was love struck over. Hell, we coulda been shot by our own patrols, but instead he got shot by an NK patrol and I hit the ground, but they found me."

He noticed me sipping my mug. "Any more of that coffee?"

"No. Want me to make some?"

"Yeah."

He continued his story in the kitchen.

"Anyway, so Bill is dead and I'm prisoner of the North Koreans. Pisses me off to think about it, John. I'd been through some hellish battles. We chased the damned NK's from the east coast of that country all the way to China and I survived every fight. Lost the tip of my finger from a ricochet, but other than that I was unscathed. Then to get dragged away because of some pussy starved rube... well, it's my own fault. I was a rube myself. I made the decision to go with him."

He followed me back into his relaxin' room.

"Did you read about the General?"

"Yeah. How did you know where he'd be?"

"I didn't. I was a know-nothing regular in the infantry, but I guess because of how they got me they thought I was something more. They gave me to the Chinese right away."

He kicked off his shoes and extended the chair to the full recline position, staring at the ceiling.

"Two years later, I find out Van Fleet was in that damn village almost the same time I said. An explosion went off near his convoy, but they missed him and killed a couple of regular army guys. Hell, John, I just said that to make 'em stop torturing me. Just my dumb luck that what I told 'em turned out to be nearly accurate. That's what put me in Leavenworth. That and being where I wasn't supposed to be in the first place. Technically, I was AWOL when the NK took me."

Here he stopped and I felt like I also needed a break.

"Coffee's done. I'll get us some."

"Black for me."

"Ok."

I returned and gave him his mug. He brought his recliner to upright, then left it to join me on the sofa.

"Ok, Charlie," I coaxed. "The book ends when you stumble into the Eighth Army camp."

"Yeah, from there the Army started keeping their own record of events. After a few days of recuperation, they took me to a place in South Korea called Freedom Village... town's name was Panmunjom. This is where American P.O.W.'s were repatriated."

"What does that mean?"

"It means they made sure we hadn't turned Commo. It's also where we got to tell our tales of woe and where they first put together my story with the Van Fleet incident."

"Is that when you wrote all of this down?"

"No, that was here in the States. Funny, the Chinese thought I was somebody important for the U.S. and the U.S. thought I was somebody for the Chinese. They brought me up for court-martial and appointed a bright, young fella to defend me. He bought me that little diary book and told me to write down everything that happened to me when I was with the Chinese and NK's. I think he was afraid I might start trying to block out what they'd done to me once the hearings began."

"And then?"

"They couldn't prove I had any connections, so they decided I'd been sold on the Commo doctrine and that I was a potential threat to the welfare of this here country."

"But you never signed any of the Communist bullshit. How could they figure you'd turned?"

"They knew I didn't, but they needed to hide me away, just in case. They did that to a lot of us prisoners. Senator McCarthy was shooting his mouth off and scaring everybody, so the Army didn't want Congress snooping around about any of their soldiers. When in doubt, hide them away."

"And screw the soldiers in question."

"Exactly. On August 4, 1953, I was sentenced to 48 months in the Leavenworth stockade."

"Joseph McCarthy, now he was a piece of work."

"Yeah, when I think about all the loyal Americans that went to jail or were blacklisted because of that prick, it makes my blood boil and I just wanna..."

He hesitated, then tilted his head to rest on the sofa back. "I hated my country, John. It ain't so bad now, but the things that were going on then, I just kinda lost all faith in it. I suffered for three years because I loved her, but she turned on me. Threw me away like fodder. Everything I'd done meant nothing and I felt used up."

"It was scary times, Charlie, but the Constitution saved us. The courts put a stop to it and when McCarthy and his cronies fell, they came crashing down like a blown up bridge."

"Came crashing down a little late for way too many people."

"That's true, Charlie, including you, but it did come."

He pushed his butt towards the back of the sofa, then slouched his shoulders with head down, eyes gazing to the floor. He inhaled and started to speak, then exhaled without speaking. He closed his eyes and inhaled again. "John, I need you to help me defeat the Chinese."

Needless to say, I was a bit stunned by this. "How do you mean?"

"I gotta relive what you just read."

Surely he didn't mean this. Nobody could want to go through that again. "Come on, Charlie. You know I respect you. Don't play around with me."

"That's right. I know you respect me because you never ask what's wrong with me – about me shooting blanks. You never even mention it when I say those words."

He turned to stare at me with a pathetic expression of hopelessness, painfully waiting for my response.

"That doesn't matter to me, Charlie. Hell, that isn't what it's all about. I enjoy making you happy. Period."

"And for 35 years that's what I've been waiting for – you. I couldn't tell my wife. I should have, but never did. Janie was made before the war. When I got back, we tried and tried but I couldn't make any more kids, so we adopted. She wanted me to have doctors test me and I refused to do it, because I didn't wanna know. I do know, John – you read what they did to me. That's when it happened and they broke me."

"Wait a damn minute," I interrupted. "They did not break you. You told a lie to make it stop."

"True, but the mental block is still there. That damned Chinaman is still there. That's how he broke me. He won, Johnnie. I can't get rid of him. Every time I start to shoot, I think maybe this time he'll be gone, but he ain't. He's right there on the table with me, laughing at me, watching me suffer. He's still shocking me, violating me. He drained me, Johnnie. He took everything from me and I can't get it back. He won't go away. I can't make him. I need you."

Countless questions raced through my mind, but I didn't know which one to ask first. It was like I was in some sort of dream state and unable to snap out of it. It took me awhile to absorb it all, to understand exactly what it was he needed from me.

Charlie waited patiently, until I gathered my thoughts to realize he intended to rewrite his own history.

"Will we do all of it?"

"No, just the end."

"What if I hurt you?"

"You will hurt me, but we can control that."

"When do you want to do this?"

"As soon as we set it up. The stuff's in the car."

There was no way for me to deny him. He had lured me into his nightmare. He had chosen me to be his savior and the only solution was to release him from his deeply ingrained torment. Pvt. Charles Higdon had suffered long enough.

"Tell me what to do."

I followed him to the garage. We brought in an electrical generator, a metal bucket and plastic bags from the hardware store filled with ropes, wires and clamps.

"We'll use the bedroom."

We peeled off all blankets and sheets, leaving only the bare box springs and mattress between brass railings at the head and foot of the bed. Then, he led me to the basement, where leaning against a wall was a large sheet of plywood. Once we got it up the stairs and to the bedroom, the plywood was just slightly longer and wider than the mattress. I helped him lay the sheet of wood on top to simulate his torture table, then Charlie grabbed me by my shoulders.

"Go in there and open the book. Count to pages 34 and 35. Read it. Memorize it. Know your part. When you're finished, I'll be ready. Don't pay any attention to what I say, just follow the book. All you need to listen for is if I say 'printing press'. That's my stop words. If you hear them, stop everything. Reality returns. Got it?"

"If you say, 'printing press', it's back to John and Charlie, here and now."

"Right. Now, go."

Like a zombie, I did as he told me with no questions. I put his exact, written words to memory and cast myself into the role of interrogator. On page 34 of the diary, Charlie estimated he had been electro tortured off and on for nearly an hour. Numerous times he had almost passed out, but each time Wo Chin had ordered that he be drenched with cold water, then the shocks would start again.

After reading the words over and over for 20 minutes or so, the interrogator's spoken dialogue was emblazoned onto and into my brain. I was ready. Passing through the bedroom door, I stepped into a time warp. The year was 1951.

Before me lay the victim, stretched spread eagle with clamps attached to nipples and testicles. Ropes were tied to each corner of the bed posts and one by one I tied the other ends to his wrists and ankles. On the floor was a bucket of water. I poured it over his body and watched it cascade over him, off the edges of plywood and to the floor below. Then, I stepped to the generator. He had taped to it a handwritten note. *When ready, turn dial to 2 and flip switch.*

I flipped the switch and my prisoner bolted from the shock, back arched, fists clenched and toes curled. I hovered over his tormented face.

"You Americans seem to think you are superior. Perhaps we will see how much of a man you really are."

Climbing onto the sheet of plywood, I crawled between his thighs and positioned myself. "Now, we will attack your manhood. You do not respond to pain, so we will torture your penis."

I lifted the flaccid organ in my hand, then covered it with my mouth. I brutally scraped with my tongue to trigger its growth. The prisoner let out a mighty groan through clenched teeth.

His cock was reluctant to respond and this caused me to nearly panic. The longer I failed to bring him an erection, the longer he would have to endure the voltage, so I spit it out to say my next part. "How does it feel to have your masculinity taken from you? You will perform like the man you pretend to be."

Again I orally attacked him, frantically working on that triangle. This had to work. It always worked. I tried to ignore his tortured body, his anguished grunts and groans, but I was terrified, wondering how I could have allowed myself to become involved with this. What if something were to happen? A heart attack? Permanent damage to his brain? Any and all possible disasters raced through my head, as I continued to assault him. I was within seconds of calling it off when I finally got a response. Mercifully, his organ started to swell and every inch of expanding meat simplified my task by giving me more of him to stimulate.

With his penis fully erect, Charlie continued his script. "God... damn... you... don't... do this... to me."

I removed him from my mouth, "I will drain you until you talk. Only you can stop what is happening to you."

My oral stroking resumed, while the voltage continued to rack his body. He writhed in an electrified dance, as his vulnerable peter was mercilessly assaulted.

"Never. You'll... never break me."

I released the organ to speak, "You create your own pain. How much more would you like?"

Taking my scripted cue, I stepped to the generator and turned it off, then raised the level to 3. The victim collapsed, frantically struggling for air. I sucked his dick some more, demanded he talk some more.

He hurled an insult my way. "You... sick bastard."

My script told me to return to the generator and flip the switch. Now the victim's screams were constant with each agonized exhale of breath. He arched his back and thrust his mighty chest even higher into the air, as I again slaved away on his throbbing penis.

Relentlessly, I scraped and stroked, while the tortured man writhed beneath me. His entire body shook, as he withstood the unholy voltage raging through him. I let go his cock.

"Talk, Higdon. It is your only escape."

Between the manly groans of excruciating pain, the prisoner remained defiant, "I... will never... say it... you... sadistic... son of a bitch."

The page had ended and so had my speeches. I crushed his dick in the back of my throat and resumed stroking up and down, side to side. I willed him to end this, attacking him with a gusto and energy never before known to me. With every ounce of strength I could summon, my tongue and mouth licked and scraped, begging the man to finish 36 years of misery. And then a nearly inhuman, tortured voice pierced the air.

"Ugh... choke on this... you... Commo FUCK!"

He came. Charlie released ungodly bursts of semen into my throat. I couldn't take it. For the first time in my storied, successful, man-pleasing career, I could not consume what I had brought forth. I gulped and slurped as fast as I could, but excess amounts dribbled outside my lips and down the outside of his shaft. Charlie's organ contracted repeatedly, each time firing another unfathomable stream of his long-lost seed. All the while, electrical current raged through him, forcing his spine to remain arched, chest thrust high into the air and every muscle flexed to capacity.

While it was truly mesmerizing to see this ultimate definition of masculinity exhibit his powerful body beneath me, at the same time his suffering nearly brought tears to me. My motivation was the triumph – the end of his struggles – which sealed our unification forever. Together, we had eradicated 36 years of heartache, of unbridled frustration and hopeless defeat. I had played my role and helped him to rewrite the ending to his story. No longer would the guilt he had carried for so long prevent him the complete, ecstatic pleasures of orgasm that every man deserves.

His departing words to Wo Chin were exclaimed between frantic inhales of air, as his body was pushed to the edge of endurance.

"Gag on it... you... piece of shit... you... will... never... break... me."

Wo Chin had taken every drop Charlie could spew and so did I. Finally drained, his cock was laid to rest on his belly and I leapt from the bed. Standing next to the generator, I waited for his signal. Charlie was looking at me, still tortured by the electricity, but smiling as though the weight of the world had been lifted from him. It was. Wo Chin was gone forever.

"Printing press."

Part Five - Our Passion

My first goal was to get those hideous clamps off of him. Next, I untied the ropes and helped him from atop the plywood to stand, but he was a bit unsteady.

"I better lay down awhile, John."

I guided him to the floor and put him on his side, grabbed a pillow for his head, then joined him face to face. The carpet was soaked with water, but neither of us cared. Charlie's eyes were half closed and mouth opened just enough to flash the top teeth. He was smiling, still breathing heavily and gazing at me.

"We did it, John."

"We sure did." I wrapped my arm over him and massaged his back. "An explosion for the ages."

In silence, we stayed there with eyes locked on one another for untold minutes. I listened to his breathing return to a relaxed pace, while my fingers slowly ran up and down his spine, gently pressing into the tortured muscles. Eventually, his eyes closed and he drifted away from me, so I left him there and maneuvered the plywood off the bed. After the sheets were again on the mattress, I guided Charlie to stand up and lay on its softness.

I put towels down around the bed, brought him a glass of water and forced him to sit up and drink it. All that should have been done had been done. Charlie and I fell into a long, deep slumber.

For the remainder of the weekend, this is where we stayed. Little by little, we cleared the room of all the paraphernalia, while in between we consumed meals, had a cigarette or two and tended to hygienic needs, but all other minutes were spent either sleeping together or loving one another in that bed. Charlie performed with the passion of a man in his 20's, producing impressive amounts of semen each time I called on him to enter me wherever he wanted. I was also orally entertained numerous times, as his confidence and skills easily matched my own.

It was dark when one of my many explorations found me kissing his chest. My tantalizing journey led me to his stomach and belly, where I tongued the rim of his navel and saturated the hairs surrounding it, and as I stumbled onto his semi-erect penis and kissed him there, Charlie's hands and fingers gently encompassed my noggin. He guided me down the length of his shaft, until my lips made contact with his forbidden testicles. I delicately kissed them. He said nothing, but maintained control of my head with his hands. I nibbled on small chunks of their skin. He released my head, widened his legs and brought his feet up to cross his ankles atop my back. Charlie groaned with pleasure, forced me to lie flat with my arms tucked underneath me, then removed his feet from my back and opened himself in a spread-eagle posture. My marathon of testicle worship began, and as the intensity of my tongue and lip assault increased, Charlie drew up his legs and opened them like the wings of a butterfly.

For the first time, Charlie's orgasm came from the touch of my hand, because my mouth remained on his nuts throughout the ordeal. My fingers did on occasion bring his cock down over the tops of them, but this was merely to moisten it. With thick layers of my spit for lubrication, I hand-stroked his penis while munching his testicles. Together, Charlie and I eradicated the final remnants of his pain. It is true that he had been broken, just like he said, but no more. He was once again 100 percent man and he was 100 percent mine.

At the end of the month, Charlie's home became my new residence. It was his idea for me to write the book and it became another form of therapy for him. Each day he would read my drafts, helping me to edit and insert his own flair for words. His story was enhanced with a colorful, blue-collar dialogue that only he could give it and the end result is pure Charlie. It is his book, his triumph.

Like most Korean War veterans, Charlie is now in his 70's. He long ago retired from the newspaper, while I am supported by both my writing and by him. Despite his age, he has not slowed down either mentally or physically. He remains an overwhelmingly dominant force when we are horizontal, while continuing to be the best companion anybody could ever hope to have.

Sometimes he gets angry at the current political situation and I think it stirs up those old resentments in him – says it's McCarthyism all over again. He's right about that, but with the Soviet Union gone the new enemy is the Internet and television and music and video games and film and all this supposed immorality. As before, the crusaders claim their divine right to persecute based on 'protecting the children'.

"Bullshit," Charlie says. "It's the parents' job to decide what their kids can do and see, not government. Besides, isn't there a war going on? They should be committing their full man power to that issue, not this one."

He sees witch hunts aimed at free speech and independent thought and it make his blood boil, until my prodding helps him to step back and look at the big picture.

"You know how it works, Charlie. The right-wing pushes us to a certain point, then people get fed up with it and we kick them out to the gutter. The pendulum starts to swing back to the middle. Just wait until 2006. Let's see how many of those self-righteous dicks get thrown out on their ass. It'll be like the backlash of the 1960's."

"Yeah, you're right. We just gotta ride it out."

"2008 will be even more fun. That's the beauty of the United States Constitution. It only allows one side to get away with so much, then the courts take over and tell them to shut the fuck up and leave the people alone, until we can get to the polls to have our say. Balance of powers, Charlie, the rights of the individual, that's what you suffered for. Just keep believing in that document and it'll take care of us little guys."

Dialogue such as this usually leads us to the bedroom, where we reinforce the love we feel for both our country and each other.

FROM ON HIGH

Antinous was an obscure figure nearly forgotten, nearly overlooked by the all-knowing Zeus, but not quite. His distant bloodline to Crius, a Titan, doomed him to the fate of all Titans, those who had opposed Zeus in his victorious battle to rule the world. Antinous was cast down from Mount Olympus, damned to eternal torment.

The method of punishment was determined by his physique, for when the eyes of Zeus fell upon him, the mighty God was filled not only with undeniable intimidation, but also with an uncontrolled rage of jealousy. Masculine beauty in its highest form was Antinous, every muscle, line and curve of his physique a marvel of precise engineering, perfectly designed to stimulate and mesmerize both male and female observers, regardless of whether those observers were gods or mortals. To male deities, Antinous was a threat; to female, he was a temptation. Therefore, Zeus banished him from Mount Olympus, gifting Antinous to the mortals below.

He was chained to an altar of stone, placed naked in a temple dedicated to Gaia, the goddess of the Earth. The altar was a half sphere, a dome, and onto its highest curved surface was placed his buttocks. His limbs were stretched tightly in four directions to form a backward curving X. The heels of his feet and fingers of his hands were but inches from the floor of the temple, while his phallus, the strong, sturdy, diametrically flawless tool of manliness, was given to perpetual rigidity. It stood to an exact, vertical erection, majestically piercing the air, reaching for the heavens. And framing this glorious penis below its shaft, two perfectly rounded testicles lie in wait. Pulsating with energy, these balls were full of life, charged to the ceaseless production of masculine seed. This endless flow of semen, a continual fountain of come, was to be extracted by any and all who worshiped in the temple of Gaia.

Such was the decree of Zeus; this, for Antinous, a never-ending torment, his eternal fate.

The temple was surrounded by agriculture, by groves of the

olive and fig, by vast fields of wheat. The people of this valley praised the benevolent Zeus for his gift to them. They praised him by milking the unfortunate Antinous. In groups large and small, they would arrive to first place their offerings of plump olives and figs upon a table of sacrifice, then lubricate themselves with congealed animal fat taken from a container beneath. Thanks was given to Zeus and Gaia, as each man and woman surrounded the altar to absorb the beauty of its bound victim.

The ultimate glory of masculine perfection was chained before them. A downward stretch of his legs and feet sloped on one side of the apex, his upper torso on the other. His head was turned to welcome all who entered, eyes glazed with a hypnotic lust. His arms strained against the chains that bound him, fists clenched tightly, causing the powerful chest to protrude dramatically outward, while his rippled belly caved inward. Exaggerated exhales further flattened the belly and expanded the chest, as he tempted them to move near, to closely scrutinize their gift. Despite the draping and stretching atop the domed altar, he gallantly arched the lower spine, tensing every glorious muscle to accentuate his mesmerizing form. And flexing atop the curved stone, his powerful buttocks thrust a mighty, fully engorged cock directly upwards, the pinnacle of this framed image which greeted all visitors to the temple.

His body was ravaged and praised from head to toe – the skin constantly glistening with his sweat and their spit. While others licked and tasted the masculine Titan, each man or woman, one by one would manipulate the ultimate penis, extracting his seed and utilizing its bountiful, benevolent powers.

Men would climb the dome to impale themselves upon his rectum filling cock. They drained the semen and absorbed it, infusing the gift to their blood and muscle. Men became possessed of a strength and durability unknown to them. Not only was this evident by the increased efficiency of their work, but also by the incredible maximization of their libidos. Men found they could satisfy their partners with godlike erections and never-ending streams of manly come. Women mounted the dome to insert the Titan's heavenly tool into their vaginal walls, coaxing it to ejaculation. The ingestion of his semen increased their female fertility, charging their organs with an invigorating acceptance of selective sperm soon to come from their husbands. When the men fucked their women, only the most prized spermatozoa were allowed entry for fertilization. Because of this, females of the valley produced the healthiest of children – infants of amazing stamina, perfectly suited to work the groves and fields of crops. Oral extractions of Titan sperm also were performed by males and females, the resulting semen swallowed, taken to the fields and groves, and then regurgitated onto the earth. The seed of Antinous fertilized their valley to produce incredible yields, increasing year by year from one growing season to the next.

This was their sacred duty, but by no means was it a tedious affair. Mounting the glorious penis of Antinous lifted their spirits to the heights of Mount Olympus itself. This mighty cock filled and stretched their innards, inflating the men with an amazing sense of strength and virility, while overwhelming the females with its dominating power. Their submissive desires were intensified and these emotions combined to solidify the bonds of each man and woman, husband and wife. Manifested by ecstatic sessions of mutual praise – exhibitions of maddening sex between them in the comfort and privacy of their own beds, the seed of Antinous filled each man and each woman with an unyielding want for his and her own partner. Sprayed by his orgasmic Titan juices, vaginas of women and rectums of men were set afire, causing all to frantically undulate and writhe atop the dome. Only when every human cavity was filled could the session of worship come to an end. Only when each had greedily tasted the fountain could they consecrate these magical powers into every facet of their earthly world.

As for Antinous, he was consumed with a ceaseless and heightened lust that could not be satisfied. Stimulation of sensitive points was magnified tenfold. The mere contact of tongue upon his nipples caused him to expand the chest and force his sensitive knobs deeper into their mouths. Wetness upon his belly made him gallantly suck in what was already flattened, further highlighting the rippled muscle to receive their tantalizing tongues and lips. The thick skin of his feet and delicate skin between his toes twitched when stimulated, as he arched and spread the toes wide to invite increased praise. Every muscle of his body tensed in a constant state of expansion, morning, noon and night. Testosterone continuously raged throughout his bloodstream. The testicles were forever engorged. His ejaculations did not lessen the pressure inside. Constantly bulging like the balls of a snorting bull, his nuts were perpetually primed to jettison their bounty through his shaft and spew from the glorious, mushroom fountainhead of his cock.

It did not matter what form of wetness engulfed his phallus.

It did not matter the number of ejaculations performed. Antinous was tortured by chained desecration, tormented with a never-ending madness. Forever consumed with his unyielding desire to erupt, he unwillingly posed and flexed in all his masculine glory, tempting and inviting all who entered the temple to finish what could not be finished. The eternal tool suffered in unholy agony, unable to escape his hell of ceaseless, yet unsatisfying, orgasmic explosions.

One generation after another reaped the bounty of this gift. The temple of Gaia was a sacred place and the people of its surrounding valley were enriched with the finest olives, figs and wheat known to the world, but, as so often happens with all things good and bad, the march of time dimmed the importance of this gift.

There came a group of men who found reason to fear the temple, or, to be precise, the writhing entity upon its altar. Jealousy consumed these men. To them, this hypnotizing form chained atop the dome threatened their manhood. Antinous was perceived to be representative of an unobtainable masculinity – a level to which these men could never rise. And so, they schemed of ways to defile him, thus lowering him to the status of mere mortal. They plotted to take his masculinity away from him.

Into the temple entered these four men: Agenor, the instigator of the plot, carrying a half curve knife as a weapon of defense; his friends and coconspirators, two brothers, Giles and Jerome; and Theron, the strongest of body, but weakest of mind amongst them, who toted the ax that would unchain Antinous from the altar. One by one, chains were severed. Their victim then was draped across the dome facedown, as Agenor climbed the slope to perpetrate his foul deed.

The glorious gift of Zeus was violated by this man's cock. He forcefully rammed his greased and engorged tool into a quivering anus, while the other three grasped limbs of their prisoner, stretching him motionless. Each of the four in turn filled the bowels of Antinous with their sperm of defilement, thus raping, and in their minds, reducing this glorious man god to the humiliating status of wasted whore.

The screams of Antinous were not confined to the temple of Gaia. His groans were not contained within the fertile valley where the temple stood. Anguished cries of the raped Titan echoed to the keen ears of Zeus, high on Mount Olympus. His rage was indescribable, punishment immediate.

Unbeknownst to them, the four rapists were inexplicably filled with an anguished lust, a madness far beyond the scope of that given to the Titan by Zeus. Taking the lead, Agenor and Giles threw the hapless Theron to the floor, grasping his ankles and lifting both legs, as Antinous, now released from the grasps of his tormentors, stood silently to observe a frenzied melee amongst the mortal men.

With cheeks spread wide, Theron's ass was invaded by Jerome, who savagely thrust his now dry cock deep into the man's rectum, brutally fucking, ruthlessly ripping him apart. Blood oozed from the ass rim of Theron, painting the fucker's cock a crimson red. Quickly, Jerome fired his seed and exited the poor man's battered rectum, at which time Giles and Agenor released both of Theron's ankles, leaving him to quiver and moan on the temple floor – but not for long.

Agenor clutched his hand onto Theron's penis. He used the recently raped man's rock hard pole as a leash, forcing him to his feet, then dragging him towards the gifting table. With Jerome and Giles watching closely, Agenor leapt to stand upon the table, curved knife in one hand, cock of Theron in the other. He kicked away all gifts offered to God Zeus, then yanked the leash, coercing his victim to lie in a prone position atop the table and on his back. After letting go of Theron's dick-leash, Agenor stood with his feet straddling the man and lustfully glared at him, stimulated by the view from his towering position of dominance.

Looking up, Theron spied two juicy nuts dangling as though they were apples on a branch, tantalizingly out of reach. Agenor spread his legs wider and bent the knees to lower his pulsating orbs, as well as his fully engorged cock, all of which were quickly devoured by Theron. He slavishly lifted his upper torso to engulf Agenor's nuts, sliming them with his tongue, sucking them with his lips. Theron's tongue laid a trail of spit which led first to the underneath of Agenor's projectile penis, then along the length of its shaft, until reaching its bulging corona, all of which disappeared into darkness, crushed to the back of Theron's throat.

Meanwhile, watching from the tableside and impatiently burning with desire, Giles and Jerome decided to launch festivities of their own. Jerome lifted one foot to rest on the table's surface near Theron's hip. He tempted his brother to enter from behind. Giles invaded with a raging-out-of-control penis that incestuously fucked the virgin asshole to oblivion, while Theron continued his slavish, oral worship on the protruding phallus above.

Two more orgasms were spewed, one into the mouth of Theron, the other into the rectum of Jerome. With no hesitation, no moment of rest, three men suddenly attacked Agenor, their leader. They draped him across the table chest down, gripping and pinning his ankles at one end and his wrists at the other. His ass was repeatedly violated first by Giles, then by Jerome and finally Theron, as each man exchanged duties of pinning and fucking, pinning and fucking.

Once Agenor was pounded into a blathering idiot, they released him, only to unleash an all-out orgy of sex. Partners were frantically exchanged. Chaos ensued.

Each man was skull-fucked. Each man was butt-fucked. Endless streams of semen were jettisoned deep inside every opening. Four cocks held firm throughout, as virgin assholes were torn to shreds. Blood dripped and smeared the youthful skin of the four men. Their frantic assaults escalated into a feeding frenzy, but no manner of brutality could satiate their desires, no lusting desecrations could appease their appetites. Unable to control their maddened yearnings, they soon incorporated the ultimate violence into their drama.

With ax, Jerome attacked his brother Giles, while Agenor put the blade to Theron. Two of the men were soon lifeless and the two remaining turned against one another, leaving Agenor chopped to bits, Jerome bloodied but still standing. He removed the blade from his fallen comrade's grip, brought it to his own throat and opened his skin to complete this macabre scene. Four corpses lie prone on the temple floor.

This became their grave. Zeus destroyed the temple around them, pressing it deeply beneath the earth and sewing the ground above to leave no trace. Only Antinous remained, but he too was removed from the valley, lifted between finger and thumb by Zeus to witness from above the final act of vengeance to be exacted.

The fertile valley instantly withered and died. Desolation and pestilence consumed all living things, and the people were left with nothing, forced to drift aimlessly in all directions and begin their lives anew.

Perhaps it would make for a pleasant end to say that Antinous was allowed his return to Mount Olympus, but this was not to be. Eternity means forever, regardless of interruptions perpetrated by foolish men.

The torture of Antinous was given to a new temple in another land for another people. There he remains, still writhing, chained to his altar of never-ending lust. His penis continuously spews its magical seed from its mushroomed fountainhead. Unequaled in beauty, unmatched in manly strength, this masculine form, this tormented Titan, is dutifully worshiped, and forever cherished by those granted

their gift from on high.

BANDIT'S PREY

Bob Taggert could sense something was different. Neither the dogs that normally patrolled the area near his house nor Marshall Nolan, the ranch foreman, were anywhere to be found. In fact, no vehicles were in sight, not even those of Taggert's two ranch hands. The only sounds were an occasional braying of cattle, while all else was quiet – too quiet. Still, the lights inside the home glowed just as Bob and his wife had left them.

"Something ain't right, Marsha."

"What do you think it is?"

"I dunno, but until I find one of the boys, I ain't taking any chances."

He parked the pickup truck and reached to the gun rack mounted on the rear window. Opening the barrel, he took a box of cartridges from the glove box and inserted two shells, then turned to his wife.

"You stay here 'til I make sure everything's ok."

"No, I'm coming with you."

"Damn it, Marsha, I said stay here."

He exited his pickup and slowly approached the house. All was silent, as he gingerly stepped up onto the porch to peek through a window. Seeing nothing out of the ordinary, he unlocked the front door, threw it open and stepped inside, but just as he did the muffled scream of his wife came from behind and a devastating blow smashed the felt crown of his Stetson hat. Bob Taggert crashed unconscious to the floor of his front room.

When he awoke, Taggert found himself lying flat on the floor surrounded by three masked men. They had removed his shirt, unsnapped the jeans and exposed his penis, which one man held in his fist, pumping to keep the organ erect. With his arms pinned to the floor by one man and legs secured by another, Bob struggled to escape, while shouting in protest to the black mask manipulating his manhood.

"What the hell are you doing? Let me go, you sons-a-bitches."

None of the three answered. Instead, the man stimulating the penis produced a thin strip of leather, then proceeded to wrap it around the victim's testicles. Continuing, he brought the ends and crossed them over the top part near the base of the cock, crossed them again on the underside, then pulled the leather taut and tied both ends together. The leather encircled both the penis and testicles to form a cock and ball ring, forcing the genitals to remain fully charged with blood.

"God damn it, what do you want, for Christ's sake?"

With nothing spoken, the men lifted Taggert to his feet, then manhandled him towards the landing of a stairwell leading to the basement. One clasped a hand from behind onto the prisoner's throat, while the other two secured his arms and pulled him in the desired direction. Once they reached the landing, Taggert shuddered at what he saw in the basement below. Marshall Nolan, his ranch foreman, was suspended by the wrists from an overhead beam. His eyes were closed and mouth agape. Stripped to his underwear, red splotches and wounds were clearly visible on his chest, belly, back and legs as he hung helplessly, seeming to be unconscious.

As the man with the choke hold roughly forced Taggert down the stairs, the captive soon saw his other ranch hands, Jason and Lucas, plus three more masked invaders. One of them held a shotgun on the two and another held a knife. Both ranchers were stripped of their shirts, while their unbuttoned pants, as well as their underwear, had been lowered to expose their buttocks. They were forced to lean with hands spread against the wall. Behind them, the three menacing figures stalked with their jeans peeled open and hardened dicks exposed.

Then, as Bob Taggert descended the final step, he was forcibly turned to his right and saw an actual face.

"Hello, Mr. Taggert. Remember me?"

His heart sank even further, as what he first feared had come to pass. "You sneaky mother fucker."

"No, I've never done that, but your wife was a pretty good lay. Hang him, men."

Bob Taggert was taken to a rope that dropped from one of the high-above rafters, at the end of which was tied a noose. They inserted the prisoner's head and tightened the knot, then secured his wrists behind the back with another rope, forcing him to stand on his toes to keep from strangling.

He struggled to speak, "Hey, my wife says a lot of things she knows nothing about."

"Oh, sure, Bob. And I'm just some rube who believes everything he hears. Look around you. In case you couldn't tell, I'm a professional thief. We prey on husbands whose wives say too much and yours said plenty."

"What she says and what's for real ain't always the same."

"So I figured. That's why we're here. You can tell us what we need to know and you can do it the easy way or the hard way. Whatever you think."

"It ain't here. I don't keep it on the ranch."

"Sorry, Bob, I don't believe you. Guess you'll have to watch us do our thing."

Taggert stood helplessly and waited. The arches of his feet already were sore, but any lowering of his body tightened the noose around his neck, so he continued to prop himself up. He watched the men bring two of his saw horses from the side wall and place them between him and his two ranch hands. With a shotgun still aimed at their heads, Jason and Lucas were forced to strip naked, then made to bend over and straddle the ends of the horses. The blond-haired Lucas cast his eyes to the floor, while Jason turned to look at his boss.

"Don't worry, Mr. Taggert. We ain't told 'em nothin'."

"It's my fault. I'm the one that brought them here. I'm sorry, boys."

Each of the men's ankles were roped to the two vertical legs of the saw horses, followed by the wrists, which were stretched beyond their heads and tied to the top horizontal beams. From Bob's view, each man's buttocks faced him about four feet away, while their bodies were bent at angles of 90 degrees. Their legs were spread like an inverted "V" in conjunction with the legs of the saw horses, while their strong backs flared from the extended and stretched position of their arms.

The lead henchman butted in, "That's a touching speech, Mr. Taggert, but we know they can't help us. They're just here for our entertainment. You can watch, too."

Removing their belts, two of the bandits started laying leather across the broad backs of the ranch hands, starting at the deltoids and working downward towards the butt cheeks. Neither victim cried out, but emitted manly grunts and an occasional whimper. Taggert watched the beatings in anger, but this rage was not directed at the hoodlums. No, Bob Taggert was angry with himself – and his wife. It had been less than 24 hours since they had last seen the man responsible for this invasion – this violence against him and his employees.

Sex had brought this to them. Bob and Marsha Taggert liked to swing with other couples. They had just wrapped up a satisfying four way in the plush room where they had spent the last two evenings – The Pepper Grinder Hotel and Casino in Wendover, Nevada.

Wendover was just a lonely spot along Interstate 80, until someone decided to put a casino there. Surrounded by the Utah Salt Flats to the east and Nevada desert for endless miles in every other direction, there was no logical reason to put anything there, but somebody did and soon two other companies came to the same area to build.

Bob and Marsha loved to visit Wendover – more Marsha than Bob – and would book their favorite room at the Pepper Grinder weeks in advance, even though there was no need for reservations. It was their destination of choice for any special occasion or just to get away, because Marsha loved to play the slots, while Bob enjoyed the comfy beds, good food, saunas, swimming pools and frequent sex parties his constantly-horny wife managed to put together for him. Plus, knowing how his wife liked to gab with strangers, he avoided taking her to Las Vegas or Reno, where too many hustlers and con-artists lurked for easy prey. The Wendover crowd – what little there was of it – was more their kind of people and this allowed Bob to relax.

His first meeting with Everett and Mindy Hurst came at the hotel pool and nearby whirlpools on an open-air rooftop. Pre-arranged by Marsha, the Hursts joined the Taggerts for a swim, then conversation in bubbling and heated water – four in a hot tub. Bob's screening process was thorough, as Everett and Mindy convincingly posed as vacationers weary of the crowded casinos of Las Vegas and Reno. He was an insurance salesman for The Prudential and she, like Marsha, a housewife. None had kids, because they preferred to party – in the bedroom – and since they were more than attractive enough, that's where the four of them ended up. Two joy-seekers and two con-artists traded partners to fuck, eat pussy and suck cock in a marathon, six-hour session.

Making the most of the Taggerts's two-king-sized-bed suite, the gala ended with some three-on-one body worship, the final recipient being Bob. They stretched him out on one of those big beds, and while Mindy and Marsha took turns riding up and down that thick pole, Everett and whichever other one was available worked their tongues all over Bob's compact and strong body, stimulating every sensitive area that could be found.

It was one of the hottest hook-ups he had ever been involved with and he performed like some sort of super-human stud, keeping that cock fully swollen and firing endless salvos into whatever receptacle happened to be ready to take it. After that, Bob and Marsha slept peacefully, while Everett and Mindy returned to the casino for more slot play – or so they said. Obviously, the Hursts had checked out of the hotel and – armed with whatever information they had finagled out of the naive Marsha – managed to find the Taggert ranch, bringing the entire gang of bandits with them.

Suddenly, a painful scream jolted Bob from these memories.

Straining his neck to the left, he saw a cattle prod electrocuting his foreman, Marsh Nolan. The suspended man howled in agony, as the metal touched the middle of his back and forced him to thrust the upper torso forward, where he was greeted by two solid fists pounding into his chest and belly. Taggert winced when he saw what they were doing to his good friend. The body twisted and writhed, uselessly trying to avoid the simultaneous assault to both his front and back.

Oddly, Bob Taggert didn't think about the ungodly pain being inflicted upon his foreman, but more about the desecration of that beautifully masculine body – one which he had seen up close and personal many times. Wiry and chiseled from hard work on the ranch, now it was being scarred by the hideous jolts and bruising punches. And as a further insult, the cattle prod was one of their own – hand-held, battery powered and capable of delivering up to 60,000 volts of electricity – used by the ranchers in persuading animals to move through chutes or up and down ramps. It was designed to prod 1000 pound livestock – not 180 pound humans. Marshall Nolan was a man and Taggert could no longer idly watch them torture his friend with that hideous device.

"God damn you, Hurst, stop it. He doesn't know anything."

"Of course not. We figured that out long ago. This is for your benefit."

"Leave him be. Let my men go and work on me."

Hurst raised his hand and the torture stopped. "Your time will come soon enough."

Nolan's body collapsed and the chin dropped onto his chest. Scars of crimson red peppered his handsomely defined shoulders and muscular back. Bob was sickened by the sight of this, as he reflected upon the times he had lovingly scraped his nipples across the solid surface of that man's back, while driving his penis into the squeezing depths of the same man's bowels.

Men get lonely moving cattle from one part of 250,000 acres to another, and since men are purely sexually beings, they have no reservations about taking care of one another next to a warm campfire miles from nowhere. These men held a deeply seeded trust and fondness for one another – a necessity on the open range, where one slip up could result in injury to either men, horses or valuable livestock. Inspired by rolling hills and natural grasslands at the foot of the Calico Mountains, these men strengthened their bonds when darkness fell.

Every 30 days or so, Bob, Marsh, Lucas and Jason would cull a number of select animals from the herd, then drive them to the feedlot pens built between Nolan's living quarters and the main ranch house. These cattle drives usually took at least 76 hours to complete and when the four men were alone at night on the grasslands, Bob would hook up with Marsh and Jason with Lucas.

This man's cattle was a prized commodity. Once the selected head were brought to the home feedlots, they would be pampered for the final year of their lives. Only irrigated corn went into their bellies and Taggert beef had a direct pipeline to all the Las Vegas and Reno hotels. In fact, all Bob Taggert needed to do when he had livestock ready for harvesting was to dial his phone, call the packing house and wait for their trailer trucks, which would be sent directly to his ranch within 12 hours. For three generations the Taggert family had run one of the finest cattle operations in the state and a check arriving from the Gerlach Postal Office would mean pay day for the Taggerts and their hired hands.

He loved these men and treated them accordingly. They had a top-notch bunkhouse within sight of the main house, plus Bob Taggert paid them in cash, because where they lived banks were hard to come by. Three hours north of Reno, the only town of size anywhere near the ranch was Gerlach and even that was 65 miles away. This is why Bob used the bank only to convert checks into cash and kept plenty of it in a safe at his home.

As for Marsh Nolan, he rarely went to town even on pay day.

He had everything he needed right there on the ranch – his own living quarters with a view of the feedlots, main house and bunkhouse; a Taggert-furnished Chevrolet dual-wheel pickup truck; plus weekend visits from his good pal and hunting companion, Brian Smith. Friends since elementary school, Marsh and Brian grew up near Puff Pucker, Nevada, a spot 90 miles away along the Southern Pacific Railroad line, where the only thing of importance was the meat processing plant where Brian Smith was employed.

Nolan's boss didn't care about these overnighters between the two men. As far as he was concerned, they were merely hunting buddies and whatever else they did when the lights went out was none of his business. Marsh Nolan was loyal to him and an essential element to the successful operation of the ranch. He inventoried the cattle, did maintenance on vehicles, equipment and buildings, plus kept the younger Jason and Lucas in line. Nolan was the perfect foreman and whatever benefits Taggert got from him on the cattle drives were just gravy. These men were too proud to let any petty jealousies interfere with or spoil the chemistry amongst them.

This is why Bob was consumed with both guilt and anger – guilt for putting his men into this situation, anger at the man instigating it. As he scanned up and down the tormented form of Marsh Nolan, he lashed out.

"That's enough of this, you son of a bitch." He hesitated, gasping for air before thrusting his body upwards with aching feet. "You came here to deal with me, Hurst – or whatever the hell your name is, so cut them loose and let's get to it."

"Ok, Bob, if you insist, let's do just that. But I will not be releasing your men. You can listen to them scream while we work on you. We'll see who can scream the loudest."

He motioned to his henchmen and the torture of Marsh Nolan was resumed. Meanwhile, the others stopped the whippings of the prisoners tied to the saw horses. Instead, two hard peckers were rammed into two vulnerable ass holes and brutally thrust to the very depths of their rectums. Jason and Lucas groaned from this invasion – not from the pain of it, but from the humiliation, this degrading penetration of uninvited cocks. Taggert watched helplessly as the backsides of both men were battered into tenderized meat and although remorse filled his heart, he also felt proud of his men. They took this violation with manly resolve, never crying out or begging the invaders to stop their brutal assault. Neither Jason nor Lucas would give these scum bags that satisfaction.

"Your face is turning red," Hurst mocked. "Do you need some air?"

Taggert's pained arches were slowly failing him. Inch by inch gravity pulled him towards the floor and as it did, the noose around his neck tightened to restrict his intake of oxygen. With a gurgling gasp, he defied the tormentor.

"Get... fucked... asshole."

Hurst approached the struggling man and clamped his fingers around the leather bound and erect cock. "Ok, tough guy. Think your hot shit, huh?"

Taggert closed his eyes and remained silent.

"Yes, you are quite the man – or so you think. Let's see what you're really made of."

Nausea hit the pit of Bob Taggert's stomach with the ferocity of a punch. It sickened him to think that this slime ball, the very one who less than 24 hours earlier had caressed and coaxed his body to perform for the ladies, would be the same man to unleash a different type of coaxing. He tightened his gut to hold back the vomit, then invited his own torture to begin, "Bring it."

Hurst ordered all punishments to stop and summoned his six henchmen. Marsh Nolan was abandoned to again hang in suspended agony, while the hired hands were left straddled over the horses with unwanted jizm oozing from the reddened rims of their ass holes.

"Take him to the bench."

Taggert was released from his noose and dragged towards the wall opposite the stairwell. There, eight feet from the wall sat eight metal file cabinets lined in a row and placed back to back, four against four. Each of the three-drawer cabinets was filled with containers holding nails, screws, nuts and bolts of every size imaginable, plus metal clamps, chains, clips, vises, wires, bonding glues, tapes and any other form of hardware you can think of that might come in handy to maintain the buildings on a cattle ranch.

Atop the cabinets rested a slab of smoothed wood five feet wide and six feet long, the thickness of which was six inches. This squared table top was the men's work bench. Suspended from the ceiling and hanging four feet above was a fluorescent-lit lamp, the four-foot long tubular kind, which was activated by a switch on the nearby wall. On that wall were shelves built to house electrical tools such as circular saws, jigsaws, battery chargers and sanders, along with hand-held screw drivers, wrenches, hammers and other special tools for whatever jobs might arise.

Hurst and his men had long ago cleared the table top and turned on the light. Now they cut loose the wrist bindings, dragged the man to the work bench and laid him atop the surface.

"Strip him."

While four held him down, the other two proceeded to pull off the boots and socks, then jeans and underwear, leaving the victim with nothing but the leather strap, which continued to keep his cock and balls fully engorged.

"Tie him up."

Four ropes were brought, looped and knotted to each ankle and wrist. Then the other ends were taken to the nearest vertical support beams, wrapped and tied to the base of each one. The spacing of these beams caused Taggert to lie spread eagle on the table. His head hung off one end, while the edge lay below his arm pits and the angle of the ropes caused his arms to be pulled downward towards the floor. At the other end, the heels rested flat on the wood surface with the ankles spread four feet apart, the same as the distance between his wrists. His body was horizontally stretched taut, but not tight, while the downward angle of his arms caused the chest to rise high into the air and abdominal cavity to sink down in a dramatic drop from the rib cage. His forced-to-erection penis lay throbbing on the belly.

With his head hanging off the table, he turned to his right to see the side view of Marsh Nolan, still suspended with chin dropped onto the chest. The eyes were closed and breathing labored. As for the boys, they remained quietly straddled over their saw horses, trails of bandit cum oozing down the scrotums and dribbling off their balls to the floor below. With their heads pointed towards the wall, they were mostly unable to see what was happening in the room, but Jason strained his neck to lock eyes with his boss, flashed a smile and resumed resting his head on the horizontal bean to await the next assault.

Suddenly, Taggert felt a hand on his peter and he lifted his head to see Everett Hurst manhandling the organ.

"Ok, Bob, I'll give you one last chance. Where's the money?"

"There ain't no money here."

"Liar. Your wife already told us there is. Where do you keep it?"

"You think I'd tell my wife anything? She'd spend every dime if I gave her the chance. What she's told and what's the truth are two different things."

"Well, the truth is what I want," he crushed the hardened cock in his grip, "So, spill it."

"I've got nothing to say to you."

"That will change."

He released the penis and barked out another order, "I want this thing standing straight up. Fix it."

The masked men found the equipment they needed in the cabinet drawers: three chains 12 inches in length, the links of which were a diameter of one-quarter inch; three metal clips; and three four-inch nails. One man attached the hardware. Using the thumb and fingers of one hand, he squeezed the organ to create a gap between its skin and the strip of leather wrapped around the base. He threaded a chain through the leather near the right side of the cock, stopping after three links had passed through the strip. Then, he looped and connected the short end to the rest of the chain with a metal clip, hooking two links together. This pattern was repeated and soon three chains were looped around the leather strip – one to the left, one to the right and one to the center underside of the prisoner's shaft. Once each chain was attached to itself and the leather strip, he held the cock vertically upright in his hand and nodded to one of the other assistants.

Taking the other end of one chain, he stretched the links until the chain formed a straight line pointing to the prisoner's right leg, then drove a nail through the final link and into the table's wooden surface. He moved to the other side of the work bench to repeat the pattern, securing that chain close to the left leg. Now, the center chain was stretched its full length and nailed to the center spot between the legs, as the other man released the penis from his hand.

The desired result was achieved – Bob Taggert's majestic cock stood tall and firm, pointing directly upwards to the light above him. Forced to erection for nearly an hour, the mighty tool shined with pre-orgasmic ooze, which dribbled from the slit to form a glowing, one-quarter inch circle around the opening. He strained to raise his head and absorb this humiliating degradation of his masculine body. The eyes focused on the pulsating, yearning penis, as it pierced the air in a vertical display of phallic glory. Testing the ropes binding him, he flexed the arms and pulled with all his strength in a desperate struggle to break free, which caused the powerful chest to expand, belly to flatten and every line of muscle to come to life.

Hurst mocked him, "Oh yes, Mr. Taggert, I can see you are quite the man."

The ropes held firm and he abandoned the useless attempt to break them, then dropped his head and prepared for the worst. Suddenly, he felt fingers surrounding his navel and he again lifted his head with the body tensed.

"You know, I do admire these rock hard abdominals," Hurst dug his fingertips into the solid surface and kneaded the muscles as though they were bread dough. "I see them as a challenge, a brick wall to be broken down."

It truly was a thing of beauty. Majestically spacious in comparison with his compact chest, the belly was thick and powerful with a deep line running from the middle of the stomach to the navel and below. Curved ridges flared from either side of the line, while a healthy trail of black fur connected the navel to the pubic hair. The belly button itself was set a far distance from the pelvis, which created a dramatic chunk of muscular meat between it and the throbbing peter. Taggert again raised the head to witness his torment, while flexing and flattening the abdominals to defend himself.

Hurst let go the belly and stepped to the side wall shelves. "Hmm, perhaps these spikes will do the trick."

He grabbed several of the wooden stakes and set them on the table. "What are these? Tent stakes?"

The victim groaned and dropped his head, refusing to answer, but the hoodlum was correct.

These wooden tent stakes were 12 inches long, with a flat head on one end, tapering to a rounded, one-eighth-of-an-inch point at the other. Finding a wooden mallet, Hurst inserted the sharp end from one of the stakes to that long surface midway between his victim's navel and pelvic bone, then with a devastating blow, brought the mallet down to strike the head of the wooden stake.

A horrific grunt exploded into the room, as Taggert strained with all his might to withstand the punishment. With repeated blows, the interrogator drove the stake deeper and deeper into the solid muscle, nearly impaling the man underneath it.

"Talk," he taunted his victim while continuing to pound the stake home. "Where is the money?"

Nothing but manly groans and grunts came from this powerful man. He clamped shut the eyes and concentrated every thought, every ounce of strength to his beleaguered belly's defense, but soon felt another spike piercing the pit of his stomach. A second henchman began to pound a second stake into the hardened muscle.

"Give it up. You cannot win."

Manly, deep throated and breathy exclamations of "Ughhh" and "Ooghhh" rumbled from the depths of his chest, but Taggert refused to speak.

With two men on each side of the table, four stakes soon formed a circle around the tortured man's belly button, as the final two were placed one inch on either side to join the one above and one below. The four men synchronized the striking of their mallets so that one four-pronged impalement after another pulverized the belly. Repeatedly, they speared the poor man's muscles, hammering each stake into him deeper and deeper.

Each blow brought raspy and ear-piercing gasps of "Aaghhh" and Uughhh," as the interrogator badgered him.

"Talk, now. Where's the loot?"

Taggert strained to withstand the punishment, as each rapping echo of wood on wood drove the stakes into the solid wall of muscle. The arms pulled on the ropes for leverage, helping him to tighten the abdominals to capacity, but a sickening nausea raged throughout his middle section and his resolve began to weaken. Adding to his misery, each movement brought sharp pains to the base of his immobilized cock, as the leather strap was held firm by the chains hammered into the table's surface. He opened his eyes to focus on the light above him, refusing to watch them torture his belly, but then a weakened voice coming from the right strengthened him.

"Hang in there... Bob."

He turned to see Marsh Nolan staring at him with a reassuring grin. Purple bruises dotted the rib cage, while bloody red scars splotched the back, shoulders and legs. "Don't give up."

After all the ranch foreman had endured, Taggert wondered how he could possibly allow these thugs to break him. With a newfound defiance, he unleashed a verbal assault. "Uughhh, go ahead, you bastards. I can take it."

Now, the contest was on. Hurst ordered the other henchman

– who had resumed using their own cum as lubrication to fuck the helpless Jason and Lucas – to turn their attention elsewhere. "Shut that one up."

Marsh Nolan was again tortured with electrocution from behind and fists pounding to the chest and belly, rendering him into a writhing, grunting and contorting slab of meat hanging on its hook. His eyes remained locked with those of Taggert, as the admiration they felt for each other strengthened them to resist their interrogators.

Taggert looked in amazement at the suspended man. Each punch smashed into the sinewy-muscled body as though it were a boxer's heavy bag, yet he never begged for mercy or cried out from the pain. His stretched and vulnerable torso tensed to capacity and absorbed these blows as though he felt nothing. Each touch of the cattle prod left behind new splotches of red on his tortured back, but he merely grimaced from the shocks, all the while staring at his motivator.

Nolan was awed by the powerful man stretched atop the table. He absorbed that compact, muscular chest as it expanded and rose high into the air, then scanned down to the long, flattened belly, inspired to see it withstand each pulverizing spear hammered down into it with devastating effect. The arms, legs, chest and abdomen all were flexed to capacity, as Nolan's hero used every muscle to take his torture like a man.

Both men smiled, focusing their attention not on their own agony, but on one another's heroic display of strength and resolve.

Seeing Nolan's suffering filled the boss with rage. "C'mon, you sons a bitches. Aaghh, is that all you got?"

Hurst took the challenge and ran with it. "Ok, fellas, anywhere between the rib cage and groin. Let him have it."

The four men moved the stakes from one area to another, pounding the pointed spears into hardened muscle ten or more times before moving to the next spot and repeating the pattern. All the while, Hurst and his victim continued their verbal contest.

"Talk, or I'll run you through."

"Do it, pussy," he watched the others torturing his friend, oblivious to his own punishment. "I'll never tell you."

Mercifully, Marsh Nolan's eyes closed and he again lost consciousness. Hurst ordered those men to leave the suspended victim and get back to the boys on their horses. All the while, he and the other three continued to pulverize all areas of Taggert's belly.

"Talk, damn you."

The tortured man once more gazed to the light above him. Each piercing blow sent reverberations from the pit of his stomach to the depths of his groin, where the mammoth cock and engorged testicles continued to throb and ooze. It took all he could do to suppress the urge to vomit, so he focused his attention on the mighty penis itself. Raising his head, he gazed past the ever-moving and impaling stakes to admire the strength and beauty of his own organ. He marveled at the shiny syrup that coated its bulging crown and relived all the ecstatic orgasms – those with his wife, those with Marshall Nolan and yes, even those with the two con-artists back in that Wendover hotel room. With an explosive exclamation of anguish, he shouted at the perpetrator of this horrendous assault, "Suck my dick, you faggot."

Suddenly, everything stopped. Taggert collapsed his head and gasped for air, struggling to replenish his battered belly muscles with oxygen, but before he could even begin to recover, two leather soled shoes with rubber heels were grinding into his abdomen.

"Who are you calling faggot?"

He looked up to see Hurst standing crouched on his middle section. "My name is Malcolm Flowers and I ain't no queer."

He grabbed the suspended light fixture and swung it away from the table, then held it there, stood upright and began violently jumping on the man's belly. "I am a professional. I do what is necessary to achieve my goals."

The victim tightened every muscle and watched in amazement, as the face of this raging madman turned beet red.

He continued to leap up and land with both shoes grinding down into flattened muscle. "I am the best in the business. You will be broken. I will have what is mine."

Taggert knew he had touched a very sensitive nerve in the interrogator and so, to further antagonize the man, he smiled as though nothing was happening. "Well, Mr. Flowers," he taunted in phrases each time the maniac leapt into the air, while grunting each time he came down, "you sure know... *ughhh*... how to get... *ooghhh*... a fella off... *uughhh*. Are you... *ummphhh*... sure you... *ooghhh*... ain't a fag?"

No longer Hurst, but Malcolm Flowers leapt two more times before realizing he had made a critical error. Not only had he blurted out his actual name, but also allowed the prisoner to find a weak spot, his deeply ingrained denial of what he was. Flowers knew he would have to suppress this inner rage and find a way to use it against his opponent. Still standing on the tortured belly, he launched a counter-attack.

"So, Mr. Big Man, think you're some sort of super stud, do you? Ok, I've seen you shoot it. Let's see how long you can hold it. You'll be begging for a cock sucker before I'm finished with you. Too bad there aren't any here."

He climbed down from the table and put the wheels into motion. "You three can take your turns on those two bitches." He shouted to the others, "You three, over here."

As the six masked men switched duties, Bob Taggert lay quietly recovering from the belly assault. His head hung off the table with eyes closed and he sucked in precious oxygen at a rapid pace, relishing in his small victory and much-needed rest period.

Flowers motioned one of the men towards him and whispered instructions, "Go upstairs and get all the bottles of rubbing alcohol you can find. Then check on Mindy and that woman while you're up there."

As the masked man climbed the stairs, Flowers scanned the labeled file cabinets until he found what he wanted. He opened the drawer and took out two boxes, then stood and pointed to the wall. "Bring that and set it up right there between his legs."

Next, he leaned over to get a close-up view of that gorgeously throbbing and oozing cock. "Bet it wouldn't take much to get you off, hot shot." He placed a fingernail onto the triangle of sensitive skin just beneath the slit, then cruelly flicked it as though shooting a marble. The powerful organ contorted from the attack in a desperate attempt to thrust towards the belly, but was efficiently immobilized by chains and cock ring. All it could do was surge with added strength and emit another discharge of pre-orgasmic slickness. It's owner groaned from this painful assault, as the tormentor taunted him.

"Must be humiliating for you – chained and helpless, stripped of everything, your entire body at my mercy and there's nothing you can do about it. I feel bad for you, but you'll just have to lay there and suffer, big man."

The basement became silent, as Flowers waited for the return of his assistant. Even Jason and Lucas made no sounds – only the animalistic grunts of the men fucking them from behind could be heard.

Taggert used this time to recuperate and wonder what had happened to his wife, Marsha, then he tried to imagine what she possibly could have told these two hoodlums back in Wendover.

She'd said she met Mindy while playing slots and soon was introduced to Everett, a.k.a. Malcolm Flowers. Obviously, she had told them the general location of the ranch and plenty of other details – at least enough for them to figure out that money was kept here, but only he knew the location of the safe. This comforted him. The future well-being of everyone important in Bob Taggert's life was now his responsibility and he promised himself he would never reveal this secret, regardless of what further tortures they might put him through.

During this recess, Flowers further prepared for the next round of interrogation. From one box, he produced two small alligator clamps, while from another he grabbed two wires. Using a pair of insulation strippers taken from the shelves, he exposed two inches of wire from both ends of each and threaded it through the alligator clips. Then, he ran the other ends to the edge of the table where a battery charger sat in wait, plugged in and ready for use. After threading the wires through the charger's posts, Flowers waited for the final ingredient.

"Hey, boss," the masked errand boy descended the stairs. "I found what you wanted."

He handed Flowers one bottle of isopropyl alcohol and one tube of Campho Phenique ointment, which is an antiseptic used mostly for insect bites or cold sores.

"Good work. What is Mindy doing?"

"She's got that woman tied to a chair in an upstairs bedroom. She put duct tape on her mouth to keep her quiet."

"Is she watching the drive-up lane?"

"Yeah, she's got a perfect view and the pistol's cocked and loaded."

With his mind at ease, Flowers was ready to go to work. He leaned over to scrutinize the bulging genitals immobilized by chains and leather. Surrounded by the tightly wound strip, the man's balls were swollen and shimmering with a deep red hue.

He placed one index finger onto his victim's right testicle and lightly massaged. Moving in small circles, Flowers covered the surface of both nuts and the stretched skin separating them. "Look at these big ol' sperm makers."

Taggert remained silently resting with head hanging past the table. Soon, he felt a cold liquid substance being applied to his pulsating balls and he raised the head to investigate, but was unable to see what was happening. "What the hell are you doing?"

"Never mind. You'll know soon enough."

The victim dropped his head, while Flowers upended the bottle of alcohol onto his fingers and slowly rubbed the fluid onto every inch of testicle skin. After a thick coating of the liquid was sufficiently applied, he stood upright and waited. Little by little, a warm glow began to consume the swollen and already sensitive orbs.

Again Taggert raised his head, "What is that shit?"

"Feels toasty, doesn't it?"

The heat continued to intensify on those besieged testicles and as the burning sensation increased, the powerful peter surged to a new strength. More droplets of pre-orgasmic syrup exited the slit and coated its glorious crown. Then, he recognized the aroma and understood why his testicles burned.

"God damn, my nuts are on fire."

"That's right. They're full of cum, too. And that's where your man juice is going to stay – trapped inside your balls."

As the liquid dried, the burning sensation started to fade, but Flowers leaned over to apply a fresh coat and start the process anew. This time, however, he laid it on thick, continuing to paint on a fresh layer before the previous had dried. Now, the fire on his prisoner's testicles was a constant, relentless torment of minimal pain and maximum stimulation, steadily increasing with intensity.

He laid quietly, not wanting the interrogator to know he desperately needed to shoot his load, but the rising temperature on his nuts was making that more and more difficult to conceal. Then, he felt a sharp pain in the exact center of his balls, first the right one and then the left, which caused him to strain against the ropes and look to see what they were doing to him.

This time, Taggert looked past his chest, past his penis and saw the battery charger, then the wires attached to the posts. His eyes followed the wires back to his groin and he knew. They had hooked up his nuts for electrocution.

He dropped the head and whispered to himself, "Jesus fucking Christ."

Flowers set the machine to the lowest possible level and sent the voltage to his victim's burning balls. Initially, the man tensed from

knowing his precious jewels were receiving this shock, but soon realized that it was a mere tingle, another stimulation to his already vibrating gonads. This caused another mighty surge from his chained penis,
as it stood perfectly vertical in its statue-like bondage. "All you men join
me. It is time we finish this."

Six men soon surrounded the helpless victim, three on each
side of him. Flowers whispered instructions to one, then moved
towards the head end of the table, stepped over the rope and gazed
into the inverted eyes of his captive.

"Will you talk?"

With an ecstatic smile, Taggert answered, "Never, you queer.
Nothing you can do will break me."

"Ok, tough guy, we'll see." He pointed to the charger, "Raise the
level by one."

An assistant turned the dial to increase voltage sent to the
poor man's nuts. Now, the swollen orbs were attacked by thousands
of ants, each one frantically crawling inside and out of the stretched
skin. Taggert began to writhe in unbridled ecstasy. His dick dramatically
contracted with dry heaves, yearning to shoot but lacking the stimulation needed to do so.

"How about now?"

"Never, you homo."

"Apply the ointment."

Another henchman took the tube of Campho Phenique in hand,
removed the lid and squeezed gobs of the medicine onto the tortured
balls. Then, he rubbed the ointment onto every inch of skin surrounding
the voltage-conducting alligator clamps. Within seconds, the temperature on the surface of the prisoner's pulsating orbs rose to a maddening height. This, coupled with the fiery ant-crawling sensation from the
electrical charge nearly drove the victim insane. Testosterone raged
throughout his body and he writhed in uncontrolled lust, trying desperately to trigger his bound penis to ejaculation, but to no avail.

Although he knew Taggert would never admit it, the body lan-
guage gave him away and Flowers could tell this torture by denial was
slowly having an effect, so he intensified the pressure.

Bending towards the prisoner's glazed eyes, he questioned,
"Your dick hurts, doesn't it?"

There was no answer, but ecstatic and deep groans with each
exhale of breath.

"Wish you could shoot, don't you?"

Still no reply, so he continued. "Your balls are so full of cum they're about to burst. Want me to get you off?"

Bob Taggert raised the head and stared at his neglected phallus piercing the air and contracting to shoot what would not come. Turning to the right, he saw the nearly lifeless body of his friend Marsh Nolan, then the battered rectums of both his ranch hands. He strengthened his resolve to answer the interrogator – both for himself and his men.

"Do what you must. You wanna suck it? Go ahead. I'll never talk either way."

With a calm and calculated speech, Malcolm Flowers prepared his victim for further degradation.

"Bob Taggert, you have maintained an erection for well over two hours. We have beaten your belly to a pulp and filled your testicles with pent up sperm. Yet, you still refuse to talk. You leave me no choice."

Standing upright to address his henchmen, Flowers shouted, "Torture this man's cock!"

Dumping the contents of the box onto the table, each man began to clamp alligator clips to the helplessly chained penis. Tiny teeth pinched the tightened and sensitive skin up and down the entire length of the hardened shaft.

Taggert raised his head and shouted in horror, "No! You sadistic fucks, what are you doing to me?"

"Your cock is mine. I control it." A menacing grin looked down upon the tormented man. "Talk now and I'll let you shoot."

"No... never... I can't..."

Twelve alligator clips soon covered the penis from just below the crown to just above the leather binding around the base, as it continued to throb and point upwards. With fiery stimulation still being unleashed upon his nuts, Taggert's mighty cock relentlessly contracted to shoot, but only sticky syrup exited the slit. He alternated between looking at his desecrated penis to dropping his head and contorting in uncontrolled ecstasy. Taken to the ultimate heights of pain and pleasure, he cried out in a desperate plea for mercy.

"Stop torturing me. Let me shoot."

"Talk first. Then you can shoot."

"God damn you. Finish me, now."

"You are in no position to give me orders. What happened to the big stud I knew? Not so tough now, are you?"

Taggert was nearly driven insane by these conflicting emotions of pain and pleasure. Despite the unholy pinching of the alligator clamps, his amazing tool remained strong and yearning to fire its rocket, but the final stimulation would not be granted to him – not until he gave up his secret. How much more could he take? How much more would he be forced to take?

"God damn, I'm gonna explode. You've gotta get me off."

"Ha! Fat chance."

He left his victim to writhe in denied agony, stepped to the side of the table and grabbed a clamp. He attached it to the vulnerably stretched left nipple, which caused the agonized man to raise the head and flex his mighty chest. He looked at the evil teeth biting into the sensitive and erect tip, then turned to the interrogator.

"Uughhh, you sick fuck! I'll kill you... ooghhh, you hear me? I will kill you!"

With the tube of ointment in hand, Flowers gobbed his finger and applied a layer of Campho Phenique to the right nipple, while the victim continued to glare first at him, then to the tormenting finger and back to Flowers.

"You sadistic piece of shit. Not my tits... Please!"

"Don't worry. They'll get used to it."

The warm, then hot medicine started taking effect and as it did, Bob Taggert began to experience sensations never before known to him. It was as though the raging fire had penetrated the tip of his nipple and entered the bloodstream. As Flowers continued to apply one coating after another, the bound man suddenly felt as though he was everything the interrogator had mockingly named him – tough guy; big man; hot shit; super stud; quite the man – Bob Taggert was sensing himself to be all of these and more. He arched the back and thrust his nipples high into the air, inviting – even begging for more of this maddening stimulation. He had become some sort of super-charged male animal – the manliest man ever born, so he flexed the muscles, sucked in the belly and postured in a dramatic display of masculine lust.

Reaching across the chest with his right hand, Flowers took the clamp between finger and thumb, then delicately twisted back and forth to further stimulate his prisoner's left nipple.

He coaxed in a soft and loving voice, "You are one hell of a man, Bob. Why don't you talk so I can get you off? You know you want to."

Anguish consumed the man's face. His tormentor was driving him to an ecstatic insanity. Never before had he felt so powerful, so virile and masculine.

Intensifying the pressure, Flowers continued the nipple punishments and verbal persuasions, "Look at your body, so strong, yet so helpless. Only I can help you. Only I can give you what you must have. Tell me."

Taggert arched his back even further to thrust the nipples into the air, then gazed down to his throbbing penis. The entire crown was coated with a sugary frosting of dried and fresh pre-cum, while the massively thick and powerful shaft majestically contorted and caused the brutal, but stimulating clamps to wiggle up, down and side to side.

"Why are you doing this to yourself? Can't you see your magnificent organ? How can you deny its yearning? All it asks is that you allow for its release. Let your penis shoot its manly seed. Why do you refuse your glorious cock this pleasure?"

Taggert was lost in the utopian ecstasy perpetrated upon him. "Please, finish me. Let me shoot."

"You know I cannot do that without the information."

"No... don't make me... please... let me..."

He collapsed the head in anguish, while Flowers took his victim even further into this maddening torture of denial. He left the man's nipples and motioned to his henchmen with a calm tone, "In between the toes."

As the voltage stirred the nuts and clamps pinched the cock and nipple, more teeth were placed on the delicate skin between the tortured man's toes, then onto the soles of his feet. The initial pain quickly subsided, as the nerves became numbed, which left behind new sensations of incredible, testosterone-raging masculinity. Bob Taggert writhed and flexed, striking the pose of a manly hero. He curled back his toes and invited more clamps onto the soles of his feet, which the tormentors kindly provided. Flowers returned to apply another layer of heat to the nipple.

"What kind of man are you? No man can take this, not even a he-man like you. God damn, Bob, what are you waiting for?"

"No more, please..."

"Why won't you give me what I want? If you do, I'll give you what you want."

"I... can't... please don't make me."

With one final alligator, Malcolm Flowers pushed this poor man to the brink. The thumb and fingers of his left hand opened the stretched navel and the teeth of another clamp bit into the knot of the belly button. Immediately, reverberations rippled from the navel to his scrotum, causing Taggert to suck in the middle section, raise his head and cry out with a pitiful pleading.

"Oh, my god... I can't take anymore. Finish me... Please, Mr. Flowers..."

"Now will you talk?"

"Yes... please... I'm begging you... Finish me and I'll..."

"You will tell me about the money?"

"Please... get me off... then I'll tell you."

"No, no, I am sorry. First you talk. Then you get off."

"Oh, god... I can't take it... I gotta shoot now... Please, Mr. Flowers."

"I cannot help you. I am sorry."

"No!"

Another coat of Campho was plastered onto the nipple, as Flowers hovered near the man's anguished face. "C'mon, Bob, let me finish you."

The heat began to drive him wild with lust, pushing him closer to madness. He thrust the mighty chest high into the air and gazed at the gloriously tortured nipples. "Ooghhh... Ok... I'll talk..."

Flowers twisted the clamp on the other nipple. "Well?"

Taggert violently turned his head side to side with one final and desperate attempt to keep his secret, but to no avail.

"It's... under..."

Just then, his eyes happened to lock with those of Marshall Nolan, whose lips moved to form three magical words: *I love you.*

He closed his eyes, envisioned a night by the campfire and thrust his aching cock into the depths of the man's bosom. Instantly, a volcanic eruption spewed his heavenly seed straight up into the air. The first volley struck the overhead lamp to sizzle on the heated tube. Successive spurts jettisoned vertically skyward, then became a creamy flow of white lava, encasing his glorious mushroom crown and cascading downward amongst the torturous alligator clamps.

Flowers and his henchman stood in awe of this spectacle with jaws dropped and heads turning in disbelief. Mind over matter – Bob Taggert had once again thwarted these invaders, which caused the lead bandit to clasp both hands to his head and shout in horror, "You god damn son of a bitch! No man can do that. What kind of man are you?"

Consumed with rage, he began to unleash a furious assault of fists to the man's stretched and expanded ribs. One blow after another was combined with the rantings of a madman, "You... will... talk. No man can do this to me. I... will... beat... you... until..."

Suddenly, the air was pierced by an even angrier, whiny and bitchy voice that echoed from above.

"Everett, what the hell is taking so long? I'm getting bored up here."

Flowers turned to see his partner in crime on the stairwell landing. "God damn you, Mindy. Get your ass back up to that room."

"I shoulda known you couldn't break him. He's more man than you'll ever be."

"You fucking whore. He was about to talk before you interrupted. Now get the hell out of here and do your job."

"All right, all right. Why don't you do yours? You wuss."

As she turned to leave, a loud pop rang out. Mindy stood motionless for a few seconds, then turned towards the stairs. Malcolm Flowers and his six masked henchmen stood in silence to see a red dot centered on the woman's forehead, then watched as she fell forward to tumble down the stairs. Dumbfounded, they remained motionless to see her lifeless body come to rest face up on the basement floor, particles of brain and blood oozing from underneath her head and onto the concrete.

Then, in rapid-fire succession, six more shots rang out and six masked men fell dead on the floor where they stood, each with the direct hit of a bullet through their chests.

"Don't move, mister. Put your hands up."

Malcolm Flowers did as ordered.

"I've got him, Marsha. Get that shit off of your husband."

She ran down the stairs and cradled his head in her arms. "Oh, my god, Bob, what have they done to you?"

"Help Marsh. You gotta get him down. He's in a bad way."

The shooter barked to the man in his sights, "Mister, unplug that machine."

Flowers pulled the plug and removed the clamps from Bob Taggert's balls.

"Now, get over here and let that man down. And I mean you better do it nice and slow. I don't know what the hell you've done to him, but there's gonna be a price to pay."

Taggert looked to his wife with longing eyes. "Honey, see if you can set the boys free. Then they can help you with the rest of it. Get the pocket knife out of my jeans. They're on the floor over there past the table."

Soon, Jason and Lucas cradled Marsh Nolan in their arms and gently laid him on the floor.

"All right, mister, now lock your hands behind your head and stay right there. Don't make a move or I'll blast ya."

Jason addressed the gunman, "Damn, Brian, are we glad to see you."

"Is Marsh gonna be ok?"

"I dunno. They shocked him pretty good. Probably oughtta get him to Gerlach soon as we can."

Nolan lay still with his head in the arms of Jason. Groggily he opened his eyes and mumbled to the young man, "What happened?"

"Brian's here. Come to save us all."

"Marsh, you ok?"

He looked up to the landing and saw his sharp-shooter hunting buddy. "Yeah, Brian. I think so. Let me rest awhile."

"Lucas, run upstairs and get him some water."

After his wrists and ankles were cut free, Taggert helped his wife remove the hideous clamps from his body, then she delicately cut the leather strip binding his cock and balls. The tortured genitals released their pent-up blood, but remained partially swollen from the horrendous ordeal. She did not ask what all had happened on that table and Bob wasn't offering to discuss it, instead shouting to the man who ended it all.

"Hey, Brian, how'd you know there was trouble?"

"Phone call. I was in Reno playing poker at the Cal-Neva and my cell went off for one ring. I saw your number and called, but got a busy."

Lucas returned with wet cloths and a glass of water, then both boys comforted the still weakened ranch foreman.

Bob was puzzled about the phone call, "Brian, I didn't call you."

"I did," Marsha piped in. "I saw them hit you on the head and

I dialed Brian's number, but that bitch Mindy opened the door and shoved a pistol in my face, so I just dropped the phone."

As both Taggerts removed the final alligator clamps, Bob jumped off the table, forgetting about his tortured genitals. "Oh, god damn that's sore." He quickly returned to sit on the edge of his work bench. "Bastards put my cock through the ringer. Give me one of those rags so I can clean off my come."

Marsha leaned in close to inspect the damage, then ran up the stairs to retrieve ice packs for his swollen penis and testicles. Bound for nearly three hours, a purple and red lined indentation dramatized the lingering effects of where a tight leather strap had stricken him.

Brian Smith continued his story. "After thirty minutes of trying, I got a bad feeling in my gut, so I headed back to Marsh's place. Come in the back way like I always do, then I knew something was wrong when he wasn't there and his truck was. That's when I saw the dogs. Sons-a-bitches killed every one of 'em."

With the repeating rifle pointed directly to the man's head, Brian asked about the lone survivor. "So, who is this piece of shit?"

"Just a thief. Nothing more."

"You wanna shoot him or should I?"

"Nah, we'll call the sheriff. Malcolm Flowers will be a nice piece of ass for the inmates over in Carson City. Lucas, get up there and make the call."

Smith spoke to Jason, "Hey, let's chain this fella up. I'm tired of pointing my gun at him."

Soon, the hoodlum was cuffed on the wrists exactly where Marsh Nolan had been strung up and Brian safely lowered his weapon. He inspected the scarred backside of his pal, then helped him to his feet.

"Can you walk?"

"Sure. Let me lean on ya."

"Used a cattle prod, did they?"

Jason picked up the device and held it for all to see. "Fuck an A right. Now it's his turn."

"Don't do it, Jason," Bob shouted. "We ain't like that. Let the law handle it."

With his weakened pal's arm draped over his shoulder, Brian led him towards the table. "C'mon, I wanna talk to Bob."

Taggert extended a hand for a shake when the gunman was

in range. "I wanna thank you for the rescue. That was some fancy shootin'."

Brian lifted Marsh up to sit next to his boss, as Marsha returned with ice to comfort her husband. She was greeted by Brian, who wrapped an arm around her and gave a squeeze.

"Here's the real hero," he explained. "She'd untied her ropes and was headed out the front door to get her cell phone out of the truck. I got her attention and we figured out what to do."

"Yeah," Marsha joined in. "I was just waiting for Mindy to give me an opening. She is not good with knots. When she left the room, I was gone."

Brian resumed his part, "I didn't know what the hell to expect, but your clever wife hatched a plan and led me to the basement. By the way, that was Marsha who shot the woman right between the eyes. Got her own pistol out of the truck to do it with, too."

Bob was impressed. "Wow, honey, you did that?"

"I couldn't wait to blow her brains out. Bitch took advantage of me."

"Man, you've been practicing. Guess your quick thinking to dial Brian's number is what really saved us."

He watched his adoring wife tend to his damaged penis and testicles with a newfound respect for the woman. Obviously, she wasn't the naive, helpless female he had thought. When the pressure was on, Marsha Taggert was a quick-thinking, sharp-shooting dynamo who would do just about anything for her man – or to be more precise, her men. Combining this with her 24 hour a day horny libido, top-notch cooking and efficient homemaking skills, Bob Taggert suddenly felt like he was the luckiest man on the face of the earth.

The county sheriff had no problem with the frontier justice that produced seven dead thieves and one more prisoner for the Nevada penal system. Brian Smith quit his job at the meat packing plant and joined his buddies on the ranch. It seems that seeing the most important person in his life hanging there all bloodied and bruised gave him a newfound appreciation for life itself. He nearly lost Marsh Nolan and wasn't about to let the man out of his sights again. Brian and Marsh put up new living quarters designed to their liking, then helped Jason and Lucas do the same.

To show his gratitude for their loyalty to him, Bob Taggert made the four men and his wife full partners in the ranch. No longer employees, each partner worked their ass off to make certain it remained one of the most profitable operations in the state of Nevada.

Of course, Jason and Lucas were itching with curiosity for weeks regarding where the money was kept. Ever since hearing Bob come within one word of revealing the hiding place, they had been building up their courage to ask him all about it.

Jason took the lead, "Bob, I heard you say, 'It's under' and then that Flowers guy started screaming his head off."

Taggert let out a hardy laugh, "Hell, boys, that's the best part. It's under one of those file cabinets."

"You're shittin' me."

"Nope. Pull out a lower drawer and you'll see a trap door in the concrete floor. That's where the safe is."

"Right under his nose the whole time."

"Yep. Bet if he knew that he'd shit his pants."

Lucas piped in, "I'll bet he's had his shit stirred plenty of times over in Carson City."

Bob Taggert reflected on this, then gave the bandit just a bit of credit. "Tell you what, fellas, Flowers was a low-down, conniving piece of horse manure, but he had me fired up pretty damn good. Sure as hell knows how to push all the right buttons, so I figure he's making somebody pretty happy in that prison cell."

Naturally, neither Jason nor Lucas could keep this secret for long and soon Marsh Nolan heard all about the location of the safe, which instigated another conversation with Taggert.

"Think our money'd be better in Gerlach, Bob?"

"We got nothing to worry about."

"Yeah, but what if that guy starts telling some of his prison buddies about..."

"I fixed it," Bob jumped in. "Now, it's hot wired. Anybody besides me touches that combination dial and they'll be fried to a crisp. If it ever happens again, I'll just lead 'em right to it and say, 'Oh, please mister, don't take our money.' Then I'll watch 'em sizzle."

Marsh seemed satisfied with this extra precaution, but the discussion of the topic gave Bob Taggert a brilliant idea, which he first discussed with Marsha, then with the four men. As a final act of defiance, he would voluntarily revisit that basement work bench and allow them to tie him up just as he had been. Instead of clamps and electricity, five mouths and ten hands would stimulate that masculine body to make him feel just like the man he was during his insane torture session. In return, that amazing penis and those cum-producing nuts would properly service every one of his admirers.

And just to cure Marsha's occasional itch, he contracted with an amusement company to set up five slot machines with all the bells and whistles at one end of the basement. Whatever she lost came out of her pocket and whatever she won came out of the men's. No more trips to Wendover were necessary, because anything any of those folks could ever need or want was right there at the Taggert Cattle Ranch and basement play room.

LADDER OF LAMENT
Part One - The Sons of Mil

All is darkness now - I know not where I am. My mind has closed itself to the outside world, this being the last means of defense from the endless tortures inflicted upon me.

The torment began with fire. Wooden sticks were put to flame, then the hot ember tips placed upon my skin. For brief seconds did the embers press against me, while the leader taunted with his questioning. His name given freely - Mac Greene it is and he is a formidable foe. He is chiseled with powerful, masculine lines of which I would be mesmerized - were he not my enemy. I must prevail against him and await my brothers.

I am Ceremony, the youngest of three. We are the sons of Eremon and we came to this land seeking vengeance - justice for the death of Ith, our uncle. He journeyed to Ailech Neid in search of friendship between kings. Greeted with kindness and agreements, he then was sent on his way, only to be ambushed and slain with no mercy. The noblemen here are fearful of equals and destroy all who enter.

My brothers - Amergin and Emmer Finn - will come for me. Victory over these tyrants will be claimed, because we possess the sword - the Ancient Sword of Eriu empowers my brothers with druidry and unconquerable strength.

I was sent to find weakness in the defense of the fortress of kings, while my brothers assembled our friends and brethren for battle. Betrayal doomed me to capture. I was given up to the kings by our own cousin Ir, son of the murdered Ith. This revelation was given to me by my own interrogators, who have assumed my death is imminent. I will remember what I have heard.

They have invited this conflict with treachery. We - the Celts - will finish it. None of their tortures will break me.

Seemingly kind, yet heartless are my tormentors. After binding the wrists behind my back, Mac Greine whipped my chest with his long stick, all the while telling me how much he admired my strength. Mac

Cuill cordially introduced himself, then proceeded to sear my flesh with hot-coaled embers. From behind, Mac Cecht held me steadfast and complimented me on my refusal to cry out - or perhaps it was a taunt. I do not remember.

That time seems so long ago and probably was, but this was merely my introduction to their intents and purposes. From there, I was taken towards the center of the stone room and bound to a device of torture, which Mac Greine calls the Ladder of Lament.

Indeed, it is a ladder of sorts - made of wood. Leaning upright against the wall and extending 12 feet upwards, the two runners are held together by 12 rungs two feet in length. This separates the runners just wide enough for a healthy body to fit in between, especially when that body is stretched like mine is. You see, Mac Greine's ladder of lament is actually a movable stretch rack.

They lifted me up and forced my hands to clasp on to one of the upper rungs. With my chest facing outwards, the wrists were secured with rope, while my feet dangled above the second from lowest rung. Actually, the lowest rung is an axle, which is turned by a crank.

A heavy rope is threaded through two holes in the axle, both ends of which were bound to my ankles. As the crank is turned, slack in the rope is removed, stretching my body taut. Once I was secured to this device, the interrogation began anew.

Standing at an upright angle of 25 degrees, my body was racked with pain, as the powerful Mac Cuill turned the crank to tighten my stretching. Attached to the other side of the axle, a saw-toothed, circular gear was locked with a pin by Mac Cecht to keep my body at this tension, while Mac Greine repeated his demand for the sword.

Every joint and tendon felt as though it would rip apart, but I remained silent. Only groans of agony were heard, as I withstood their punishment. Then, one tooth at a time, Mac Cuill turned the axle. I could almost hear the creaking of bones each time the metal pin clanked to lock the gear and my body pulled further apart. The pain overwhelmed me and, nearly broken, I feigned unconsciousness to strike fear into them. My death with no information given would mean death also for the three Mac's.

Mercifully, this trickery proved to be successful, because Mac Greine relented and ordered my stretching to be lessened.

Although my victory was small and temporary, it filled me with pride. My defiance and resolve had surprised even me and the tormentors themselves seemed to be somewhat in awe.

Soon, I felt the ladder being moved and I opened my eyes. Mac Cuill and Mac Cecht were taking me away from the wall and towards the center of the room. Once there, the ladder was positioned horizontally and turned over, leaving me on the underside of the device. To my right, two massive blocks of stone rose five feet from the floor. Each was squared with a smooth surface on top and separated from one another by about nine feet.

The muscular men lowered the ladder, until the runners of each end rested on the corresponding slab of stone. Suspended underneath, my body was still stretched, but gravity pulled the middle towards the floor in a painful arc of the back. To increase this gravitational pull, a rounded stone of nearly 40 pounds was placed into the small of my back.

The ladder of lament was now used in reverse to torture me. Each time the axle was turned, more slack was given to the rope and my pelvis would inch closer to the floor beneath. Mac Greine's questioning never stopped, while horrendous pops and snaps echoed throughout my spine. But still, his torments were answered with only groans and grunts, as my resolve held firm.

Whether the three Mac's were frustrated at my defiance or stimulated, I cannot tell. What I do know is that the next assault was upon my manhood.

From below, I felt two tongues touching my exposed nipples, still tender from the beating of the stick. With wrists tied to the ladder above me, my chest was majestically stretched and expanded, arcing towards the floor. The attack of tongues intensified and I felt so vulnerable - so alone. My entire body was at their mercy and the sudden humiliation overwhelmed me. Yet, somehow, I also felt a peculiar surge of masculinity, as though I was some sort of he-man.

I struggled to suppress this emotion, because I had no intention of satisfying their desires. The third tongue, however, nearly drove me to madness. With the stone bearing down on the small of my back, I felt a wet and rough scraping across the pit of my flattened stomach.

Soon, the tongue was drenching all areas of the mercilessly stretched abdomen, saturating every inch with warm spit. This amazing tongue somehow found its way into the belly button itself, even though the skin certainly was closed shut from the arcing of my back. It dug in deep and my entire body was jolted from the incredible sensation this navel worship created.

Despite every mental effort I could devote towards restraint, this combined attack upon nipples and belly stirred my penis. I felt the blood surge into the organ, as it dangled helplessly below. Exposed to their torments, my penis was taken into mouth and forced to full erection, further humiliating and degrading me.

Now, taking turns in their pecking order, the three Mac's proceeded one by one to orally stimulate this manly organ and bring me to orgasm. While the other two licked and massaged on my chest, belly and nipples, the third would greedily drain me of orgasmic fluid.

In succession, three times did I perform for them, not once crying out from the humiliation I felt or the agony of my inverted stretching. Instead, I allowed myself to enjoy their oral praise. They brought me to a height of masculine pleasure never before known to me and I welcomed this stimulation, mainly because it kept my mind from focusing on the pain of their ladder of lament.

Once they were satisfied that I had no more sperm to give them, they removed the tongues from me and renewed the interrogation. To assist them, a new instrument was brought to bear against me.

From below, a long wooden stake was positioned on the floor directly beneath my hanging abdomen. One end of this stake had been inserted into a wooden box, which had a hand crank on one side. As the crank was turned, the stake began to rise towards me. Contact was made with the tightened area between navel and pelvic bone. Once there, the pointed tip started to grind in to me like a corkscrew.

As gravity and weight of stone forced my belly down, the stake drove into the depths of my bowels. Mac Greine intensified his demand for the sword, repeating the question over and over, until I thought my head would explode. The crank was turned again and again, driving the stake deeper into tightened belly muscle. I flexed and writhed with all my strength, while the pointed and dagger like stake continued to rise and further pierce my belly. Then, just when I thought it would completely run me through, my mind took over to defend me. No tricks this time - I mercifully lost consciousness.

With my torso arcing downward, stretched and impaled, I have suffered for god knows how long. I no longer feel this agony, however, as my brain has completely numbed the senses. As I tell you this tale, my body floats freely in a world of peaceful bliss.

But now, a distant commotion has reawakened me to the pain

of this torture. Elation! Victory is near - my brothers are near. I sense this.

Once I am free of these tormentors, revenge will taste sweet. Two Mac's will die by the sword, while the third - namely Mac Greine, will suffer as I have suffered. He will be stripped and fired embers will mutilate his flesh, as they did mine. Then, I will take my vengeance upon our dear cousin, who so jealously betrayed me.

Because he degraded me and because I am enamored by his manly body, Mac Greine will be kept alive for many days - perhaps forever. His penis will be drained and body desecrated until I am satisfied. Yes, the Ladder of Lament will be revisited and I may never be fully satisfied, so pity him.

We brothers three - Emer Finn, Amergin and Eremon, the sons of Mil, are proud Celts and we will conquer this land to have as our own. We will take what and who we want and do with them as we please.

The rest of the story is told in third person.

Part Two - Eremon's Revenge

When Emer Finn and Amergin burst into the torture chamber, they were shocked at the scene.

Immediately, they lunged to strike down the three Mac's, who were without weapons. Mac Cuill's belly was run through with sword, while another blade punctured the throat of Mac Cecht. Blood spewed in all directions and Emer Finn raised his sword to strike Mac Greine, but was interrupted by the tortured brother, Eremon.

"No - leave him! He is mine."

Following his brother's order to spare this man, Emer Finn checked his sword and left the point touching Mac Greine's throat, while Amergin bound the interrogator's ankles together and wrists behind the back. Then, after countless hours of suffering, the stake was lowered and Eremon was released from the Ladder of Lament.

As he lay in his brothers' arms to slowly recover, the obvious questions were asked.

"Success?"

"Yes. The fortress is ours and all the leaders dead or locked in cells."

"Where is our cousin Ir?"

Amergin and Emer Finn looked at each other, puzzled, until Amergin answered, "We have not seen him. Is he here?"

"He is the one who betrayed me. Find him. He is within these walls."

"What have they done to you?"

"Never mind that for now. Just find Ir and bring him to me."

The brothers exited the torture chamber, leaving Eremon and the bound Mac Greine alone. No words were spoken, as the still naked Eremon approached the tormentor and struck his face with a back-handed slap. Then, he dragged him towards the corner, where the pit of fire was carved into the stone floor.

Still silent, Eremon backed the prisoner against a nearby support column and secured him by wrapping rope around the man's waist. Once this rope was knotted, the threat was given.

"Prepare yourself, Mac Greine. I will return for you."

The interrogator stood alone, now a prisoner in his own chamber of torture, while nearby, the blood of Mac Cuill and Mac Cecht stained the stone floor a deep purple hue.

Mac Greine shuddered to think of the fate awaiting him. How many men had he broken with his brutally efficient Ladder of Lament? Now, he suspected that he would also know the agonies of this device and wondered how he would stand up under torture.

Would he break down and beg for mercy or death, as so many of his victims had done? Or would he withstand the torments with manly strength, as Eremon had done?

Mac Greine was in awe and somewhat infatuated with the mighty Celt. Eremon was the first man ever to survive such torture - never breaking, never giving up his information. From this memory, Mac Greine would find his inspiration. Revisiting the scenes of Eremon's defiance caused the prisoner's penis to awaken, but these thoughts were soon interrupted.

The door opened and Eremon entered, followed closely by his brothers, then several other men. Two of them were escorting a naked man whose wrists were bound behind him, while the remainder took up the rear. All were covered only with animal hide wrappings around their waists and their bodies bore red and purple scars of the recent battle won.

Mac Greine watched and waited, as Eremon barked orders to the entourage of assistants. The corpses of Cuill and Cecht were dragged away and soon, the ladder was again propped against the wall with the naked man bound to it, just as Eremon had been.

The room was cleared of all but the three sons of Mil and their two prisoners, as Eremon approached the naked man on the torture device.

"Now, dear cousin, explain to me why you parleyed with these people."

Cousin Ir was a peculiar sort of man - strong of body, but weak of mind. With his arms and legs stretched lengthwise on the ladder, his massive chest protruded dramatically forward and laterals expanded to such a width that they nearly were touching the runners on either side.

This strong man instantly answered the question, "For gold."

Eremon turned the crank to begin the torture of Ir. "You fool! Did you think they would honor their word - these people who killed your own father?

Ir groaned from his stretching. Powerful lines and curves of muscle were highlighted across the bulging pectorals and down the middle of his stomach and belly. Like the dullard he was, he repeated, "They said they'd give me lots of gold."

Again the crank was turned, until the eerie "click" of the saw-toothed gear locked the axle. "You gambled and you lost, cousin. I have suffered. Now, you must suffer. Your agony will be multiplied ten times and nothing you can say will stop it."

After one more sound of metal pin clanking with metal gear, Eremon and his brothers left their cousin alone to suffer on the ladder. Manly groans rumbled from the depths of his mighty chest, as it heaved and strained against the pressure of the horrific stretch rack.

Now, they turned to Mac Greine, still bound to the stone column. Eremon gently ran his hand along the chiseled lines of his prisoner's chest and belly, savoring the smooth, soft skin and sinewy muscle beneath.

"You are a fine specimen of masculinity, Mac Greine. So soft, yet so strong, it is as though you were carved from marble. Just as I once was."

He violently grabbed one of Mac's nipples and nearly twisted it off. "Look at me! Look at my chest and belly. You have mutilated my skin with fire, so this too will be your fate - eye for an eye, my friend. Brothers, strip him."

The ropes binding him to the column were cut and Amergin yanked away Mac's loin wrapping. Then, the ankles were cut loose.

"Now, take him to the pit!"

The fire was stoked and, while Eremon held his prisoner from behind, Emer Finn whipped the chest, nipples and belly with a long, wooden stick. Soon, Amergin held his own stick, but one with a heated tip, which he put to the flesh of Mac Greine. The two brothers struck the torso of this man in the same areas where marks dotted Eremon's skin. And so, the ex interrogator's burns soon matched those of his former prisoner and both were equally scarred from this mutilation by fire and whipping.

Taking his guidance from Eremon, Mac Greine refused to cry out. He took the painful burning like a man, matching the resolve he had witnessed in his prisoner. Eremon was impressed by this defiance and slowly began to realize why his interrogators had treated him the way they did. The sights and sounds of a man standing up to such punishment stimulated him, just as it had them. He plotted the next phase of his revenge.

The two brothers were given instructions to move cousin Ir. They carried the ladder and placed it to rest horizontally on the two pedestals of stone, but this time, the device was not turned over and its victim was left facing the ceiling of the torture chamber, still tightly stretched.

While Emer Finn and Amergin maneuvered the ladder, Eremon removed his loin wrapping and remained standing behind his victim. He wedged his phallus in between the butt cheeks of Mac Greine and whispered in his ear.

"You notice I did not mutilate your backside, my friend?"

For the first time since becoming a prisoner of the Celts, Mac Greine spoke, "Nor did I yours. Why is this?"

"You will know in due time."

He could feel Eremon's penis increasing in strength, as it rubbed against his soft skin. Remembering the beauty of this organ, which had been in his mouth at full capacity not so many hours ago, Mac's own unit began to inflate in anticipation of the degradation to come.

Even though he did not yet know what form of torment would be used, just the thought of this powerful man having complete control over him excited Mac Greine and his penis reacted in kind.

With the ladder now positioned upon the slabs of stone, Eremon was ready to prepare his second prisoner for further punishment - alone.

"Leave me, brothers. It is time I exact my revenge. Bar the door and let no one enter."

Amergin and Emer Finn did as they were told, locking the door behind them and posting a guard, who was given explicit instructions not to allow anyone into the torture chamber.

Still clasping onto Mac's bound arms, he guided him towards the ladder. Once there, he cut the ropes from Mac's wrists and told him to clasp his hands to the rungs above. Mac Greine obediently reached up, finding an available area on one rung between the ankles of the man being stretched and another between his wrists. He latched on to each, while Eremon bound Mac's wrists with rope - one at a time.

Looking about the room, he found a vast supply of rope hanging on the wall and, using a sharp bladed knife, proceeded to cut small pieces. Soon, he had two lengths wrapped around Mac's ankles and knotted each one to form anklets. Then, taking a long rope, Eremon threaded it through one anklet and pulled the man's leg towards one of the stone pedestals. He looped the rope around the base of the stone and pulled tight, then knotted it. Duplicating the process on the other leg, he attached that rope around the other pedestal. Now the legs, along with the arms, were spread far apart.

This left Mac Greine suspended in the shape of an "X" and his feet inches above the stone floor. Throughout the entire process, the victim never struggled or protested, while his penis waited in a semi state of readiness. For reasons he could not explain, Mac Greine trembled with anticipation, seeming to almost invite the torture to come.

As for Eremon, the view was nearly hypnotic. On top of the ladder and laying horizontal was Ir, his powerful body racked with pain. Brutally stretched, the mighty chest rose high into the air. Then, at the end of the sternum his abdomen dropped like a cliff, as the rack separated the rib cage from pelvic bone.

He struggled to breath, which caused his flattened belly to rise and fall at a rapid pace. Manly grunts and groans reverberated throughout the stone torture chamber, growing ever louder from the agonizing pressure of tendons and joints pulled to the brink of separation. Highlighting this, sweat had formed to give his skin a glistening sheen and beads of it dripped to the floor below.

Some of this sweat also dripped onto the man underneath. Mac Greine's sinewy, muscled physique was vertically stretched. Suspended with arms and legs spread far apart, his manly phallus and testicles dangled helplessly - isolated, half engorged and begging for attention.

To intensify this drama, the "X" shaped man was sucking in his belly and flexing the chest, tempting and inviting the Celt to torture and degrade his vulnerable body. Eremon's own penis was throbbing with uncontrollable lust - lust to inflict more pain upon the stretched man above and to unleash a savage molestation upon the suspended man below.

He moved to the ladder and reached up. With all his strength, he slowly turned the crank, until the magical "click" was heard to lock the gear at an increased tension. Torturous howls of agony reverberated throughout the room, as the rack brought more pressure on the powerfully muscled victim.

These sounds drove Eremon to an ecstatic madness, which he released with a frenzied assault upon Mac Greine. Moving behind the suspended man, he savagely attacked the expanded chest and belly with rough hands and fingernails. He pressed the clawed fingertips deep into muscle, stopping to ruthlessly scrape and pinch on the man's pitifully stretched nipples with his nails.

Mac jolted from this sensation, throwing back his head and tensing every muscle. His penis instantly surged to full strength, expanding and lengthening to protrude straight forward and pierce the air. What he had secretly longed for so many hours ago had finally come to pass. Now, he was helplessly bound and tortured by the very man he had so lustfully punished. Justice was close at hand and the thought of his own suffering nearly drove him insane with anticipation. He longingly begged to the masculine beauty behind him, "Take me."

Eremon positioned his throbbing unit in between Mac's butt cheeks, found the portal to the anus and drove his spear home. Like a pile driver, he rammed his cock deep into the victim, mercilessly sending it to the very back of the anal wall as far as it could possibly go.

Mac Greine's entire body shuddered from the incredible tool penetrating him and, as manly groans, grunts and howls of agony echoed from the torture above, animalistic screams and exclamations of pain and pleasure echoed from the intercourse below. This combination of masculine sounds quickly brought the dominant Celt to the brink of orgasm.

With his hands and nails frantically attacking the suspended man's nipples, chest and belly, Eremon performed a relentless dance of twisting, thrusting and battering of the victim's rectum. He rapidly drove his tool into the depths, then retracted and plowed his way into it even deeper. The frantic pace intensified, until a shower of orgasmic fluid flooded the prisoner's bowels. Manly sperm erupted from the mighty organ, completely filling and fulfilling every aching desire of the quivering man's anus.

As the mighty tool relentlessly speared him with ramrod accuracy, Mac clinched his rectal muscles to intake every drop of this man's seed. His own penis throbbed in front of him, oozing pre orgasmic syrup from its slit to tantalizingly dribble down to the stone floor.

He prayed that the powerful man inside him would never leave, but Eremon's contractions began to subside. He lessened the pace of his thrusting, until finally, he drove the spear in deep one last time and held it there, allowing the victim to crush the manly tool and efficiently drain it of all it could give.

Then, just as violently as he had entered, Eremon yanked his weary penis out of the prisoner's anus, paying no regard to the man's sensitive and battered rectum.

Mac Greine's head dropped and the chin rested on his chest. Even though he was overwhelmed and exhausted from the savagely dominant attack, his penis continued to throb and beg for attention. With Eremon still standing close behind in recovery from this physical exertion, Mac pleaded with him, "Finish me."

All the while, gut wrenching moans and howls of misery emanated from the man on the stretch rack above. He began to beg for mercy.

"Eremon, please... forgive me... I'll do anything...just let me go."

These pitiful, hopeless pleadings excited Eremon no end. He circled to stand in front of his suspended victim and greedily smiled.

"Two men at once begging for things only I can give them. What should I do about this?"

The unholy sounds of torture continued to fill his head and he was consumed by this newfound power - this masculine superiority. Grasping Mac Greine by the chin and staring into the longing eyes, he answered, "You will be finished when I say."

Then, he looked above. "Sorry, cousin. Now is not the time for forgiveness."

Eremon summoned the guard to unlock the door, then left the torture chamber, abandoning Ir to endure his suffering on the rack. Below him, Mac Greine remained suspended, while his fully charged cock continued to throb and slowly ooze sweet syrup to the floor.

Below the ladder, a purple hue of dried blood now glistened on the stone surface, frosted over with the sweat of torture and drippings of manly discharge from a penis denied.

Part Three - Welcome to Your Future

Both brothers accompanied Eremon when he returned to the torture chamber. All three sons of Mil were naked and they approached Mac Greine, who remained suspended from the ladder with his penis fully erect. Eremon clutched the organ in his hand and squeezed tightly.

"I have devised a new use for your Ladder of Lament, my friend. Not only will I show you, I will allow you to participate."

From above, the tortured Ir again pleaded with his cousin. "Eremon, please forgive me. I cannot take any more."

Eremon looked up to the man on the stretch rack, "I will lessen your stretching, cousin Ir, but I will never forgive you."

Then, he ordered his assistants to duty. Mac Greine was cut loose from his suspension, then Eremon led him towards the wall. Next, the men lifted the ladder and turned it over, gently lowering it to again rest on the stone pedestals.

This left Ir beneath the device still stretched, but with gravity forcing the middle of his body to sag towards the floor. He howled from the added torture of the arcing of his spine. After a smaller ladder was brought from the wall and propped against one of the pedestals, Eremon led his prisoner up this ladder with penis in hand. Once there, he instructed Mac Greine to lay horizontal upon the Ladder of Lament, which he did without resistance.

Eremon released his prisoner's organ, then crawled to kneel on the man's belly. "Grab hold of a rung, Mac Greine."

Just as before, the willing victim obeyed every command. He was completely enraptured by the handsome Celt and prepared to endure whatever torments were to come, as his oozing cock continued to pulsate.

While Eremon secured the man's wrists with rope, his brothers threaded a second rope through the holes of the axle, then knotted each end to Mac's ankles.

The stage was set. Eremon descended to the floor and taunted poor Ir.

"Now, dear cousin, you will feel the pain you have caused me."

He reached up to turn the crank. On top of the ladder, the tension increased and caused Mac Greine's naked body to be stretched. Below, the tension lessened and forced Ir's naked body to droop down. The curve in his spine was increased, as gravity pulled him towards the floor. Then, just as had been done to Eremon, the 40-pound stone was placed into the small of the man's back, applying even more pressure to his tortured spine.

"This is what your greed cost me, cousin. It is only the beginning."

Ir cried out in unholy agony, as his back was nearly broken in two. Underneath, his massive chest was stretched to capacity, with powerful muscles expanded and tightened from the forearms to the belly. Cascades of sweat drenched and dripped off of his body, while he groaned, grunted and begged for release.

"God, Eremon...stop... torturing me. I'll do... anything you say. Just cut me loose... PLEASE!"

With a breathy, sigh of "Ughhhh", Ir collapsed into a state of semi consciousness. The pace of his breathing increased and a slight grunt was heard with each exhale.

Eremon felt no sympathy for his cousin. Instead, he wanted to worsen the agony for both men. He reached up to turn the crank one more click, causing Mac Greine's stretching to be increased and Ir's back to further arc.

On top of the ladder, Mac began to emit small whimpers from the pain of his torture, but withstood the punishment with his penis still fully erect. He waited and longed for Eremon to worship his cock in this helpless state, even though he had no intention of begging for the orgasm.

Pointing to Ir, Eremon gave the order, "Brothers, he is yours. Drain him to your heart's content."

The suspended man was ruthlessly assaulted with lips, hands, tongues and mouths. His dangling cock was forced to full erection, then savagely sucked to orgasm. While one brother orally engulfed the victim's mighty tool, the other brutally manipulated his massive chest, horrifically stretched nipples and tightened belly. Alternating their duties, Amergin and Emer Finn took turns bringing the victim to orgasm again and again, as he uselessly moaned from both the pain and humiliation of this attack upon his manhood.

He drifted in and out of consciousness throughout the ordeal, but this did not shield him from the all consuming degradation that he felt. Whatever dignity he had left was stripped away, as the brothers relentlessly molested every inch of his manly physique.

Meanwhile, Eremon climbed the ladder and joined Mac Greine atop the stretch rack. Straddling him with knees positioned on the runners, he took the hardened penis into his mouth and began to worship.

Mac let out an ecstatic moan of satisfaction. Finally, his denial was coming to an end.

Eremon slavishly praised the phallus, wrapping his tongue around the thick, meaty tube, while sliding the lips from head to base. Touching the sperm filled testicles with his fingers, he felt them preparing to contract and jettison their fluid - then he removed the penis from his mouth.

Mac Greine looked up in horror. "No! Why did you stop?"

"You are not ready."

"Yes. Yes, I am ready. Finish me."

"I'll try."

Again, Eremon took the pulsating tool into his mouth, brought it to the brink of orgasm - then released.

Mac Greine looked up again to see Eremon grinning with a sinister cruelty. Then he knew. His torture was not merely to be stretched, but to be driven insane with denial.

He pleaded, "God, Eremon... don't do this to me."

"That is what you wanted me to say when I was tortured. Isn't it?"

"Yes. Please let me shoot."

"I never said it. Did I?"

"No, Eremon. You are much too strong for me. I should never have tortured you. Get me off now... Please, finish me."

"I'll try."

But of course, Eremon did not allow Mac Greine to have orgasm. Each time the poor man was on the brink, the penis was abandoned, leaving its owner to beg and plead for release.

And so, simultaneously, the man below was repeatedly drained of his masculine fluid, while the man above was forced to hold his. Exhaustion overwhelmed the victim under the ladder, while the unfortunate above felt as though his scrotum would explode.

Combining this torment with the unholy pain of suspension below and stretching above, both men cried out for an end to their suffering, emitting guttural groans and howls of agony.

The sights and sounds of these opposing forms of torture stirred Eremon to an animalistic savagery. He reveled in this scene, as the thought of his total domination over these two powerful, yet helpless prisoners galvanized him to inflict more punishment. His desire was to render these once proud and defiant men into whimpering wretches.

Shouting to his helpers below, he began the final phase of his plan. "Brothers, there is a box with wooden stake over by the wall. Bring it and put the stake to his belly."

It was done. Emer Finn and Amergin planted the tip of the stake midway between the man's navel and pelvic bone. "Now, turn that crank until I say stop."

The stake began to impale its victim from below, just as it had done to Eremon's belly. The stone on his back pushed from above to worsen the pressure and Ir was awakened from his semi consciousness. He reacted with horrendous grunts and cries of anguish.

"No... Eremon... I can't... take anymore!"

"You will, cousin. Just as I did."

The victim's body began to convulse and flex, as the stake ground deep into his belly muscles. Seeing this reaction, Eremon was satisfied. "That is enough. Stop."

Then, he turned to Mac Greine. "This is your fate, my friend. You have felt your last orgasm. Never again will your penis fire its deadly weapon."

A pitiful groan came from below, causing Eremon to return his attention to cousin Ir. He could see droplets of blood on the floor below the man's face, as the impalement ground his innards to a pulp.

This sight further stimulated Eremon's thirst for vengeance. He crawled up to the face of Mac Greine, lifted the head and rammed his pulsating cock into the man's mouth. Violently thrusting to and fro, he forced the stretched man to orally service him. All the while, he taunted the victim.

"You are here to serve me. It is the only reason you are still alive."

Gurgling sighs and convulsions came from below, caused by the hemorrhaging insides of the impaled man. Hearing this, Eremon furiously attacked the mouth of Mac Greine, gagging and choking him with his mighty tool.

"You tortured me and got nothing. I am a MAN... something you will never be."

This self motivational taunt, coupled with the gurgling death throes coming from below, brought Eremon to an ecstatic fury. He shot an ungodly salvo of sperm into the tortured man's mouth.

Mac Greine coughed and spewed the fluid in all directions, as Eremon continued to ram the organ to the back of his throat. This relentless, dominating attack overwhelmed Mac, causing his penis to throb and bounce on the belly, flinging pre cum and desperately seeking stimulation, none of which came.

Eremon's insatiable craving for vengeance slowly subsided. He fired the last volleys of sperm, gave one final thrust to the back of the man's neck and yanked the organ away from its servant. Fully satisfied, he ordered all torture to stop.

"Lower the stake and cut him loose."

Cousin Ir was released and brought to the floor. Unconscious, he lay spread eagle and face down in a pool of his own sweat and blood, gasping for air with a sickening, vibrating wheeze.

Eremon let go the head of Mac Greine and allowed it to fall back to the ladder, where he continued to cough and choke from the incredible load he had been forced to consume. All the while, his own penis remained rigid and ready to shoot.

As he backed away and prepared to descend from the Ladder of Lament, Eremon stopped to tease the victim one last time. He lightly flicked his tongue onto the head of the denied cock, causing it to spring up off the belly like a jack-in-the-box. After watching it bounce a few times and come to rest where it started, he cruelly left it lying there to suffer.

"Welcome to your future, Mac Greine."

The hellish revenge of Eremon was ended - for this day. Both Mac Greine and cousin Ir were kept confined, bound and naked in their own private cells. All personal needs were attended to there, but on days of torture they would be returned to the chamber. Once there, both men would revisit the Ladder of Lament.

Mac Greine was outfitted with a cast iron covering strapped to his penis and testicles, which prevented him from making contact with his constantly- aching genitals. A small hole at the rounded tip allowed him to urinate, but the device was never removed. Only when he was brought to the torture chamber would his cock and balls be taken out of the darkness. Eventually, Mac Greine remained in a state of erection 24 hours a day, as the pressure from his denial increased with each passing minute.

On the one year anniversary of the conquest of the sons of Mil, Eremon finally allowed Mac Greine to shoot his load, but it was an unsatisfactory orgasm. The tortured cock was manually stroked but three times. Although this triggered the eruption, the penis was abandoned to fire by itself with no friction whatsoever to complete its pleasure.

And so, the proclamation made by Eremon had come to pass: "We brothers three - the sons of Mil, are proud Celts and we will conquer this land to have as our own. We will take what and who we want and do with them as we please."

TORTURES OF THE DACIAN WARRIORS
Part One – Tettius Fuscus

"Bring the prisoners to me."

They entered single file – seven men stripped to the loin cloth and flanked by 10 Roman guards. Forced to shuffle in their leg irons and chains, the prisoners were made to descend a stairwell, stop in a line and turn to face the man now responsible for their care.

"So, these are the mighty Dacians."

With a wave from their commander's hand, the five front line guards stood aside, while the other five remained behind the captives, swords at the ready.

The Roman paced the line to inspect his property, as each prisoner stood tall and proud with wrists roped behind their backs. They thrust the chests forward in defiance, as the man continued to berate them.

"You are Dacians no more. Your days of plunder and killing are no more. Now you belong to Rome and your Emperor Trajanian has given you to me."

He paused to stare at one of his prisoners. This particular man seemed to temporarily mesmerize the Roman commander, as he scrutinized the finely chiseled physique and long, blonde mane.

Shaking himself back to the task at hand, he approached this man.

"What is your name?"

With a snarl and curled lip, the warrior answered, "I am Ammatas, son of Decebalus, king of the Dacians."

"You give information freely, young Ammatas. Why?"

"We do not fear you. Our people will fight you to the death, until you leave our homeland."

"Your fortress city of Sarmizegetuza will soon fall. Trajanian and his legions have successfully surrounded it. Your king has fled and we want to know his whereabouts. He must negotiate our terms for surrender. You must give up your king Decebalus and return what you stole from us or all of your people will be slaughtered. What say you men? Who will be the first to speak?"

A deafening silence befell the room, as all eyes turned to Ammatas. Defiantly, he gave his answer, "Do what you must, Roman. You'll get nothing from us."

"I will get plenty from you – in due time. I am Tettius Fuscus and I will be conducting your interrogation. You will tell me of the hidden treasure you have taken from us over the years and you will also reveal the location of your king."

Tettius continued his speech, while pacing back and forth in front of the silent prisoners, "Which of you will tell me? Do not be afraid. I will protect you from the others. Speak up now. Anyone?"

All seven of the proud Dacians stood silent with eyes forward, none of them willing to betray their king. Tettius knew they would not and he relished their defiance, for you see, this man enjoyed the game of torture. He had devised many innovative and cruel ways to extract information and his success rate was quite impressive, regardless of a man's strength or loyalty.

Besides this, Tettius already knew more about them than he was telling. These were seven of the Dacian warriors whose constant sniping and raids of Rome's northeastern settlements had plagued the empire far too long. They were members of an elite unit, one into which only the strongest and best were allowed.

Well versed in cunning and skill, fiercely loyal and extremely efficient, these seven were indeed a prized possession. Their years of fighting together had made them a cohesive team. Living in the wilderness for months at a time had made them rugged and fit in both mind and body. All were powerful specimens of masculine strength and fortitude, so Tettius knew they would not be broken easily, but he was looking forward to the challenge at hand.

"Look about the room. Some have called this my chamber of recreation, but make no mistake it is my chamber of torture. Every devise you see here is designed to create unbearable pain."

Indeed, the room was intimidating. Dark, cavernous and depressing, each wall plus the ceiling and floor were made of inlaid stone. Rectangular in shape and encompassing 200 square feet, the distance from floor to ceiling was 22 feet. Countless chains were hung from the ceiling and bolted to the floor, while numerous wooden tables, ropes, crosses, racks and other threatening instruments of different shapes and sizes dotted the room.

In one corner of the dungeon was dug out a 10 foot square pit. Three feet deep, this was a pit of fire and around the perimeter lay several metal spears and branding devices of various shapes, the ends of which were heated to the color of bright orange. Small pieces of chopped wood stacked into a corner were used to stoke the fire. Recessed into the wall, a stairwell led to a stone ledge 10 feet above the pit and overhanging part of it. Eight feet wide, this ledge continued to a heavy wooden door, which was the only way to enter or exit the torture chamber.

"Save yourselves. Talk to me with words now or screams later – the choice is yours."

He halted his pacing in front of a different prisoner, scanning the man's form from head to toe.

"You must be Telum. The elder son of King Decebalus. I have heard amazing things about you."

Whereas the physique of Ammatas was chiseled, sleek and built for speed, the body of Telum was made for power. With broad shoulders, massive chest and thick limbs, this man appeared as a glorious statue, the ultimate definition of masculine strength.

Tettius queried him with genuine curiosity, "I hear you can lift a full grown oxen upon your powerful shoulders. Is this true?"

"Yes."

"Oh, so you are the strong and quiet one. You look powerful, but I doubt any man could do it."

"I have done this and I will crush your skull with one hand if given the chance."

"You will not have that chance. We will see how strong you are when I am finished with you."

Moving behind Telum's brother, Tettius ran his fingers through the long, reddish blonde locks and spoke softly, "Tell me, Ammatas, where is our gold?"

With a sudden and savage scream, the prisoner turned and made an attempt to sink his teeth into the forearm of Tettius, who deftly stepped to one side. A Roman guard from behind pierced the skin on the back of the chained man with point of sword to quickly subdue him.

Tettius bellowed with sarcasm, "Yes, a fire burns in your belly. This is good, my fiery friend. You and your brother will watch the others go before you. You alone will be responsible for what happens to them – starting with that one."

He pointed to the man at the end of the line, "Take him to the bell."

As the prisoner was dragged away, Tettius set the wheels of interrogation into motion, "Leave the brothers with me. The rest shall be crucified until they talk or die."

Five of the guards led the shuffling prisoners out of the dungeon to a slope inside the Roman fortress, where four wooden crosses in the shape of † lay waiting for them. Meanwhile, Tettius led the procession towards the place of torment for the fifth of their Dacian comrades.

Part Two - Torture of the Bell

Two guards dragged the prisoner near a side wall of the stone dungeon. Cutting the ropes that bound his wrists, they transferred his hands to a single overhead iron ring suspended from above by chain. Once the ring was opened and then clamped shut around the man's wrists, a third guard turned a crank on the side wall to lift the arms further above his head. This continued, until the arms were stretched tight and feet dangling above the stone floor, ankles still bound by leg irons and chain.

With the wrists joined close together and arms stretched overhead, the prisoner's lateral muscles were dramatically expanded, which tapered down to the flanks and formed a powerful V shape. Tettius approached the suspended man for the final preparation.

"All men tortured in my dungeon are completely mine. It is my way."

He unceremoniously ripped the loin cloth from his victim, leaving him bound and naked.

"Lower the bell."

Two heavy chains secured to posts on the side wall supported the iron bell. As two guards released and manned the chains, it began its descent from the ceiling. The length was six feet and widest part of it three. At the top of the bell was a circular opening with metal bar intersecting it, which is where the other ends of the heavy chains had been bolted.

The single chain upon which the suspended man hung ran through this circular opening at the top of the bell, so that as it was lowered it encompassed the man's body. The descent continued, until no part of him was seen except for the dangling feet. Here the guards held the heavy chains steady and waited.

Turning to the two brothers, Tettius invited their audience, "Watch and listen, my friends."

He nodded to one of the guards. Lifting up a sledgehammer with a ball shaped metal head five inches in diameter, he swung it to violently strike the lower portion of the bell.

Metal on metal, the bell clanged with ear piercing volume, seeming to nearly shake the foundation of the torture chamber. Repeatedly, the guard banged the iron bell and the volume grew, each reverberation feeding on the momentum of the previous strike. Soon, the feet of the victim inside the bell began to contort. His toes curled forward, then arched back in a spastic dance. As the deafening tones echoed to an unbearable level outside the bell, the man inside violently swung his legs in a vain attempt to escape. Then, after 12 strikes, all motion inside the bell stopped, as the victim succumbed to the maddening, high-toned ringing that enveloped him.

With a wave of the hand, Tettius ordered the guard to lower his sledgehammer, while the other two pulled the heavy chains to raise the bell. Telum and Ammatas shuddered when they saw what the bell had done to their fellow warrior. He was nearly motionless, with the exception of the heaving chest and belly. Faint moans could be heard, as his head hung down with chin on the chest and a distinct trickle of blood flowing from each of the ears. Tettius approached him.

He shouted at the top of his lungs, "What say you? Where is the treasure... King Decebalus? Speak now, for these are the last words you will hear."

The victim stared blankly at his tormentor, but a slight upturn on each corner of the mouth told Tettius this prisoner would remain silent. He turned from the suspended man to address the two.

"He won't talk, but what about you? Will either of you save this man?"

Neither one of them said a word.

"What say you, Ammatas? Do you see the pattern? Are you prepared to witness more of this?"

He scowled at the Roman with an animalistic hiss, but gave no answer.

"Telum... will you speak?"

He stared at his tortured comrade with mouth agape, but said nothing.

"Lower the bell."

The horrific scene was repeated and again deafening reverberations echoed throughout the torture chamber. There was no motion from the victim inside the bell, as the unbearable volume intensified with each devastating clank of metal on metal. Helplessly, the two watched in anguish as blood began to drip off the toes of the poor man, starting as a trickle and increasing to a steady flow. Puddles began to form on the floor beneath him, while Tettius resumed his questioning.

"Time is running out for him. One of you must talk if you want him to survive."

Contortions filled their faces, not only from the deafening echoes, but from what those echoes meant. They knew this man would soon be dead. What they did not know is whether or not Tettius would carry out his threat to the end.

"Don't you know what will happen to him? Are you willing to have this on your conscious? You can still save what is left of him. Talk quickly, before it is too late."

The reverberations became maddening, but the prisoners stood firm. Their loyalty to the king and fellow citizens superseded the love they felt for the tortured man inside the bell and sadly, as the flow of blood cascaded in gobs, they knew.

Tettius motioned for the strikes to stop and bell to be raised. As the ringing echoes slowly began to subside, the sight of their friend nearly devastated Ammatas and Telum. The entire body was a macabre nightmare of blood. The sound wave pressures inside the bell had caused both eyes to exit from the sockets and mockingly dangle on his cheekbones, still attached to the nerves and veins leading to his brain. Purple particles of the brain itself were mixed with the giant pool of blood below him, as well as pieces of skull bone and other assorted innards.

"Pity, but at least his death was relatively quick. You two will not be so fortunate. "

The bound men lashed out in anguish. Lunging towards the interrogator, the prisoners attacked in an attempt to kill, but with wrists bound behind them and movements shackled by leg irons, their assault was easily avoided. With swords drawn, five Roman guards quickly surrounded and isolated the two, causing them to collapse on the floor in defeat and despair for the death of their fellow warrior.

They were now fully aware that this Roman would stop at nothing to achieve his goals. No amount of treachery was too great to be used against them. Coupled with their sorrow, Telum and Ammatas also realized that they would be pushed to the limits of human endurance by this vicious and sadistic man.

Tettius emphasized his point, "Now do you believe me?" Turning to the guards at the bell, he barked, "Dispose of the body and clean up the mess he made."

Tank Books

Part Three – Public Crucifixion

During the torture of the man in the bell, the other four Dacian warriors were readied for the cross. This was to be a public spectacle in open air, but still inside the walls of the Roman fortress. Once they reached the slope, the men were stripped naked and made to stretch across the topsides of their crosses, which were laying horizontal on the ground.

They were secured by ropes around their ankles and wrists, then the men ascended, as an entourage of Roman guards brought the crosses to a vertical stance.

One at a time, the crosses were lifted and placed into ready-made holes dug into the ground. The positions into which the prisoners had been bound made two of the men to be crucified head over foot, while the other two were inverted. Once each cross was secured into the dirt, the distance between the lowest part of each man and the ground itself was two feet.

Roman soldiers and citizens of the fortress were allowed to taunt and mock the naked prisoners, while prostitutes were paid in silver to further degrade them. Climbing step ladders placed in front of the men, these professionals manually and orally stimulated the victims to erection and orgasm. Wagering took place as to which man would be the first to expel his semen and which could be brought to climax with the most frequency.

This public display of cruelty served both Tettius and Trajanian well.

For Trajanian, it was a gift of welcomed entertainment for the Roman soldiers and citizens of the village. Their loyalty was of paramount importance to the stability of the Emperor's reign and this relief from their regimented lives would solidify their favor of him.

As for Tettius, he understood well the psychology of torture. The humiliation perpetrated upon these men only added to the agony of crucifixion, another tool to use against them. The shame they felt from this degradation of their manhood soon was overtaken by the real purpose of the cross – ungodly, unyielding pain. In time, this was all they could feel.

They could not hear the taunts from the crowd. They could not sense the countless oral and manual ejaculations forced upon them, because gravity became their undoing.

Gravity causes joints to separate and little by little, the gloriously naked male form becomes something from a perverse dream – something not of this world. The limbs contort and become elongated. The penis and other parts of the skin become purple, as the heart rapidly increases its paces to supply oxygen. Other skin tissue dies and organs begin to fail, because the victim is unable to support the weight of his body and cannot breath. The process can take hours or days, but the end result is always the same – asphyxiation brings death.

In words it means nothing, because for a man on the cross time means nothing. Every moment suspended there makes a man long for death, but he has no control over when it will come. Only death brings mercy from this misery.

In the case of these proud men however, there was another option. Betrayal of their king would also allow them escape. This was the choice given to them.

They suffered past the point when the crowds became bored, then beyond when the final spectators could no longer bear to look at their tortured forms. Only the changing shifts of Roman guards assigned to the slope remained. The questioning never stopped and was never answered.

Tettius was willing to wait for his information, because he was more interested with the two men confined to his dungeon. As the victims on the cross struggled, Tettius focused his attention on the sons of King Decebalus.

Part Four – The Cuspin Guard

Ammatas and Telum watched, as guards lowered the lifeless corpse from beneath the bell and removed the wrist and leg irons. Then the body was thrown into the pit, soon permeating the air of the dungeon with the foul stench of burning flesh.

Tettius was lord and master of his torture chamber. Since the time he had learned of the capture of these fierce warriors, he had been plotting the scenarios for their interrogation. That time had now come.

He ordered one of the guards to bring water, then grabbed a handful of hair and lifted Ammatas to his feet.

"You too, Telum. Stand up and I will give you both drink."

Each man quenched his thirst, while Tettius continued, "In that corner is a hole. I suggest you relieve yourselves, because I plan to keep you occupied for quite some time. Ammatas, you first."

He ripped away the loin cloth and sent Ammatas on his way, then addressed the Roman guards, "Men, I thank you. You are relieved of this duty. Perhaps you would like to join the festivities at the slope of crucifixion."

As they gathered their belongings and prepared to leave, he gave them one last order. "Send in my Cuspin Guard."

These were twelve men chosen personally by Tettius to assist with interrogations. They enjoyed their duty in the chamber and had no qualms about anything that might happen there. They were fiercely loyal to him and understood that all things he did or asked them to do was for the good of the Empire and therefore acceptable behavior.

Tettius stood waiting with sword in hand in the center of the room. He looked to see Ammatas returning from the corner pee hole and turned to Telum, "You must wait. I will take you myself, because I do not trust men such as you who are strong, but silent."

Soon, the Cuspin Guard descended the stairs and reported for duty. Their commander was a man named Emascus and he was the chief assistant to Tettius for interrogations. After the reporting formalities had ended, Tettius put the Cuspin Guard at ease.

"Welcome, men. You two, lock the door and keep it guarded. Open it only by my order or that of Trajanian, should he return. The rest of you can make yourselves comfortable, but keep your swords close at hand. These two are violent, so expect anything and everything."

As the men scattered, Tettius addressed his favorite. "Tell me, Emascus, what of the four outside?"

"One of them seems to be failing quickly, but the others remain strong and defiant."

"These prisoners here will fight us hard, Emascus. We are in for a treat. This one is Ammatas and this is Telum. I will watch this one, while you take that one to relieve himself."

With sword in hand, Emascus escorted his shuffling prisoner to the corner. Once there, he pulled on the inner thigh of Telum's loin cloth and finagled out the peter, then aimed it at the hole.

"Go."

Emascus scrutinized the phallus and felt its warmth, as urine flowed from the slit. Like its owner, the tool was thick and powerful, as it seemed to pulsate in his hand. Neither man looked to each other's eyes during this process, but Emascus quickly developed an admiration for the strength of this man and his own cock tingled a bit in anticipation of what was to come.

With his prisoner relieved, Emascus escorted him to the center of the room, then Tettius and Emascus joined the other soldiers in stripping to their loin cloths. The temperature in the cavernous dungeon seemed to be steadily rising.

"This one is Ammatas," Tettius explained. "He tried to bite me, Emascus. There is a fire in him."

Emascus circled behind, grabbed the golden locks and yanked back the man's head. "If it's fire you want, then fire you shall have."

Releasing the hair, he shouted, "On the X cross – take him to the ledge."

Two guards carried the wooden beamed cross up the stairwell, while two others followed with Ammatas. Once on the ledge, the two steadied the cross upright, as the others removed the prisoner's bindings and roped first his wrists to the two upper beams of the cross, then the ankles to the lower. Two more guards ascended the stairs carrying chains and assorted hardware.

A heavy chain threaded through a pulley near the ceiling dangled out of reach, but using a long handled fish type hook, one of the guards grabbed the free end of the heavy chain and pulled it to the ledge. On the backside in the center of the X cross was a metal hook bolted into the wood. The final link of the heavy chain from the ceiling was secured onto the hook and the guards signaled to Emascus, "He's ready, sir."

The long end of this heavy chain dropped straight down, then split into two chains, each of which was now held by two Cuspin Guards at floor level.

Emascus bellowed, "Send him."

Tilting the cross forward, they gently turned the weight of the prisoner over to the heavy chain and the men holding each end on the floor below. With his body now on the underside of the cross, Ammatas was suspended horizontally in midair with his limbs stretched in the shape of an X. Nearly ten feet directly below him – the pit of fire. Gravity pulled his chiseled form below the wooden beams, with only his ankles and wrists secured to it by rope. Hanging downward, his body appeared suspended in a midair belly flop, while the cross swung and teetered from the single hook supporting its center.

Meanwhile, near the pit on the floor below, Tettius prepared Telum for his ordeal.

"Well, strong man, we now will see if your boastful claims are true. If not, your brother will be in some difficulty."

He turned to Emascus, "You know what to do."

The prisoner was forced to lie on the floor chest up, then the leg irons were removed and his ankles locked into a wooden stock three feet long. This separated his ankles by two and one half feet. The stock held two circular rings bolted into each end outside the feet of the prisoner, with chains attached to each one. These chains came together to form a Y with a single chain, which ran up and over a pulley near the ceiling. On a side wall, the other end of the chain was threaded into a crank and when this was turned, Telum began to rise feet first.

He was lifted upwards, until his hands left the floor and he was suspended vertically no more than three feet from the pit, which warmed the skin of his backside. Two ropes were brought and tied separately around his wrists, then the other ends taken two directions and threaded through two rings bolted to the floor. These rings were twelve feet apart and flanked Telum by six feet on either side, while the placement on the floor was midway between the prisoner and the fiery pit. After they were threaded through the rings, the ropes were taken towards the men holding the two chains supporting Ammatas. Once these ropes were tied to the chains, all was ready.

Tettius squatted on the floor to meet the inverted Telum eye to eye. "Your brother's fate is in your hands. When I give the order, his weight will be given to you. Only you can prevent his fall into the pit of fire. Unless, of course, you prefer to tell me the answers to my questions. You know what they are, so I will not repeat them. What do you say to this?"

"Burn in hell, Roman."

"No, that will not be my fate, but it may be the fate of poor Ammatas."

He rose to his feet and nodded to Emascus.

"All right, men, let him down slowly until the ropes are taut."

The two men began to reverse grip on the chains, moving their hands in small increments towards the end of each chain. Ammatas descended towards the pit, while the slack in the ropes attached from the chains to Telum gradually disappeared. Telum prepared himself by locking his fingers together and stiffening his arms, as he held them close to the body with hands touching his crotch.

When Ammatas came within nine and one half feet of the pit, the ropes formed a straight line and Emascus belted out the order, "Release the chains!"

Immediately, the full weight of Ammatas and the heavy wooden cross were taken by the arms of Telum. Initially, his arms pulled away from the body a few inches, which brought his brother closer to the fire, but the powerful man quickly regained control and clamped his fists hard against the pelvic bone.

The Romans waited, taking in the view of the gloriously stretched man above and his muscle flexing brother below. Already, the skin of Ammatas was drenched in sweat, as the heat from the fire wafted up to envelope him. His sleek and chiseled chest arced downward, while the abdominal muscles were flattened to highlight every powerful line. The lowest part of him was his penis, helplessly dangling straight down and pointing to the pit of fire.

Tettius and Emascus were impressed by the sight of this youthful man, as he heroically endured the horrendous suspension from the horizontal X cross.

Tettius shouted up to him, "Ammatas... will you talk?"

"Never."

He looked to Emascus, smiled and shrugged his shoulders, "Let's see about the other one."

They circled in front of Telum, who still held the arms firm against his body. This time Emascus did the talking, "You're holding up well so far. Do you have anything to tell me?"

Focused on keeping his brother aloft, Telum merely shook his head back and forth to answer. Emascus looked to Tettius and shrugged his shoulders, "He's quite a specimen."

He nodded his head and waved the Cuspin Commander closer, "Let's take a walk."

"How long should we wait for this one, Tettius?"

"Until his arms start to pull away from him. Then we'll put him to the test."

"I am looking forward to this."

"I know. I do believe he possesses one of the most powerful bodies I have yet seen."

"We will see all of it soon."

They continued their casual conversation, while waiting for Telum to become weary. Tettius and Emascus were alike in many ways, both physically and in their mind set. Rather short, stocky and stout, their bodies were almost identical, except that Emascus was endowed with a medium thick carpet of dark hair from the chest to his toes, whereas Tettius was mostly smooth skinned.

As a team in the dungeon, they were considered the best in the Empire, because they understood that sometimes inflicting pain was not enough. Occasionally, degradation was needed to push a man past his limits and both these Romans were willing to attack a prisoner's manhood as well as his strength to achieve their objectives. They never felt any guilt or remorse for anything they did. It was not merely their job, but their duty to Rome and reputation that was important. For these things both Tettius and Emascus would gladly give their lives.

The visit eventually brought them back to Telum, whose body was now drenched in sweat. He clamped his fingers together tightly, while the inverted torso strained to support his brother.

Then, with perspiration moistening the hands, he felt his fingers start to pull apart. Once they did, all of the pressure shifted directly to the forearms, shoulders and abdomen. He tried desperately to keep the arms together, but the angle of the ropes would not allow it. Despite his amazing strength, the arms began to separate inch by inch, which allowed the suspended Ammatas to descend closer to the fire.

Telum knew he was losing the battle. The angle of the ropes pressured his arms to move both down and side to side. As the constant straining began to weaken him, he realized he would have to allow his arms to separate into a fly position. Only then could he utilize the full power of arms, shoulders, chest and abdomen to keep his brother aloft.

What he did not know was how much safe distance was left for Ammatas. The change in position would give several feet to the rope and perhaps drop his brother into the pit, but it was a risk he knew he must take.

Lessening his resistance, Telum let out a mighty groan and allowed the ropes to gradually separate his arms. Slowly, they came outside his body and downward, until his wrists were parallel with the head and one foot on either side of it.

Ammatas shuddered, as he saw and felt the hot coals getting closer. He looked down to his brother and realized what was happening. "Hang on, Telum. I am still above danger."

Actually, the crucified man had dropped nearly six feet. The change in Telum's arm position had given three feet to each rope, but now at least he had better control over the weight. The question running through the minds of both Telum and Ammatas was how long could the strong man maintain this position? More importantly, how long would he be forced to hold it?

The distance between the hanging torso of Ammatas and the pit of fire had been reduced to three feet. Trickles of manly sweat dripped onto the hot coals, as the heat below him baked the skin. Tettius in particular was intrigued by the resolve of this man. He gazed in wonder at the strong lines of stretched and glistening muscles, especially impressed with the long, rock solid belly, as each rapid exhale of breath caused the muscles to explode on its surface to form a beautifully designed wall of compact strength. Dangling alone and isolated, the victim's impressive penis accentuated his manly physique and Tettius found himself somewhat hypnotized by the sight of this helpless man.

Tettius and especially Emascus were also mesmerized by the sight of the inverted Telum. Every powerful muscle was flexed to capacity, with the upper torso resisting the pull of the ropes from each side of him. Added to this, the rings positioned behind him caused the ropes to also pull him back, except that his strong abdominal muscles fought to keep the body vertical. This perfectly engineered section of the man's torso more than amazed Emascus. He was thankful they had decided to keep Telum's loin cloth intact, as this exposed every inch of his powerful belly for viewing.

The element of time worked against him. He took long, deep breaths, desperately trying to feed oxygen to his straining muscles. They could not rest for one second, but instead were forced to constantly flex and keep Ammatas above the fire. His entire body ached and he struggled to maintain his position. Now, a new element would be added to this test of endurance.

"Which one do you want, Tettius?"

"I'll start with this one – you take Ammatas."

Emascus sprang his men into action. "Let's stoke that fire up a bit. You two, load up some stones."

Tettius squatted to the floor and met Telum eye to eye. Being near the fire, coupled with the incredible exertion forced upon him caused a glistening sheen of sweat to coat Telum's body, which further dramatized the thick, compact musculature flexing to maintain control.

"Have you had enough? Tell me of your father."

With eyes forward, Telum ignored the inquisitor and focused on his task, while Tettius glanced up to the stairwell to see two guards ascending. Each carried a heavy cargo net made of rope and inside that net was a stone. A supply of them was stacked on the floor near a sidewall and although they were of different shape and size, each weighed approximately 50 pounds. Emascus used the long fish hook to secure the heavy chain above Ammatas, inching it towards the ledge and within reach. The cargo nets were bundled together at the top and tied to a double hook. The first guard attached his hook to a link in the heavy chain, then the second placed his through the next link below, adding nearly 100 pounds to the weight on the chain. Emascus let go with the fish hook and the cross swung like a pendulum back towards the center of the pit.

Simultaneously, a groan from below and cry from above echoed throughout the torture chamber. The extra weight pulled Telum's body back nearly a foot, which dropped Ammatas within two feet of the fire. With all the strength he could muster, Telum strained his amazing belly muscles and stopped the momentum just in time. Tettius watched with eyes and mouth wide open, as this incredible man pulled on the ropes to bring his body back to nearly a straight vertical line.

It was a compromise. The added weight of the stones had initially taken a foot, but the strength of Telum had fought back for half of it, leaving Ammatas two and one half feet above the fire.

Telum's belly held firm, as both interrogators launched their verbal assault.

Emascus positioned himself on the floor at eyelevel to his victim suspended over the pit from the X cross. "Talk now. Where is your father?"

"No, I can't."

The intensity of the hot coals was nearly unbearable. Ammatas strained to lift his torso up to the cross, but it was a position he could not hold for more than a few seconds. In a desperate attempt to protect it, he mentally brought his penis to erection and clinched the scrotum to lift the organ higher.

Emascus was impressed by this display of control, but still continued the questioning. "You must talk. Your brother cannot help you much longer. Our treasure. Where is it hidden?"

"No... never."

"Think of Telum. Do you want him to carry the burden of your death? It will come soon if you do not speak."

"Never. We both will die here. Our secrets die with us."

"I cannot help you. If you wish to die, then so be it." Emascus signaled a thumbs down to Tettius, meaning that the prisoner remained defiant.

Meanwhile, Tettius was badgering his victim. "Will you talk? Where is your father?"

"No... I... Never."

"Your brother cannot hold out much longer. His skin burns even now. Every inch brings him closer to death."

Unable to see Ammatas, the strong man could only maintain his position and hope. For nearly twenty minutes his muscles had strained at full capacity. Shards of manly sweat dripped from the top of his head and hands, while his arms wavered and inched backwards ever so slowly. He knew he was weakening, but refused to give in.

"I... will not... tell you."

"How will you live with yourself? If you let your brother die, it will not be on my conscious, but yours. Speak now, before it is too late."

"He will not... die. You will never... break me."

Tettius stood and summoned Emascus. Soon, they both absorbed the scene in front of the strong prisoner.

He whispered, "I told you he was impressive, Emascus. Just look."

Inverted, suspended and arms stretched wide with wrists parallel to his head and elbows bent at 45 degree angles, the powerful form of Telum was a sight to behold. Every muscle was strained to capacity, while a manly sheen of sweat highlighted his massive chest, arms, shoulders and legs. All of his strength was pinpointed to the abdominal muscles, which bore the majority of the power needed to keep his brother aloft. Here, dramatic horizontal lines crisscrossed with a deep vertical ridge from stomach to pelvic bone and the normally inset navel pushed outward from the amazing power beneath the skin.

This scene had the same effect on both. He appeared not as a man to them, but as an all encompassing, magnificent god, heroically withstanding all that mortal man could inflict upon him.

"Yes, Tettius, he is truly amazing. Even the phallus is impressive."

"Show me."

Emascus reached up to rip away the loin cloth, exposing the victim's manhood to all tormentors.

"I fear he is too strong for us, Emascus."

"My thoughts exactly. The healthy testicles hang so beautifully, they invite torment."

The two launched an assault on the helpless man. Together, they put their hands onto the bulbous gonads, as they were stretched from the scrotum by his vertical inversion. Using fingers, they massaged, pinched and manipulated the dangling jewels. Telum's degradation had begun.

He howled from the touch of these men. "What... are you doing? You... bastards."

His protests were ignored, as the tormentors extended the manual stimulation to include the penis. They no longer were concerned with Ammatas, because they knew he was in no real danger.

Unbeknownst to the two brothers, the threat of death was never really a part of their interrogation. This was by order of Emperor Trajanian when he sent the prisoners to Tettius. Five were expendable, but the brothers were to be kept alive and unharmed. This information had been passed to each of the Cuspin Guard, who had already removed the stone containing cargo nets from the heavy chain above the cross. The two guards who had initially held the other end of that heavy chain before the ordeal began now stood at the ready to take the weight from Telum if he were to falter.

The muscles in this powerful man were numbed to the point that he did not realize some of the burden of weight had been taken from him. Not knowing the truth, he continued to support his brother on the cross, while enduring the humiliation he felt from the assault on his manhood.

The penis was now fully erect and as Tettius continued massaging the nuts, Emascus took the mighty cock into his mouth and began to suck. He slavishly worshiped the phallic masterpiece, while its owner continued to flex and strain every muscle of his glorious physique.

"Oh, god, why are you doing this to me?"

Tettius answered, "Only you can stop it. Talk to me. Answer the questions and we will spare you this humiliation."

"No. I will not do it."

"Then you will suffer."

Touching Emascus on the shoulder, Tettius signaled him to unleash a full assault on the prisoner, bringing him ever closer to an unwilling orgasm. He increased the tempo of his strokes and Telum was nearly driven mad from the opposed sensations raging through him. First, the constant strain forced upon his body caused every muscle to ache and burn. This was the torture of pain. Second, the intense love he felt for his brother seemed to somewhat numb his body. This helped him to maintain his resolve and the resistance on the ropes he needed to keep Ammatas aloft. Third, never before had he felt such praise upon his penis. The expertise of his tormentor's mouth brought him a newfound ecstasy, almost as though some sort of erotic god had chosen his cock for worship.

These out of control sensations combined to nearly cause his blood to boil. Unable to understand it, he let out a deafening groan, as his testicles started to contract in preparation – but at that moment a bizarre hissing sound came from the pit.

Releasing and stepping to the side of their victim, Tettius and Emascus watched in amazement, as the brother on the cross let go a mighty stream of urine onto the hot coals beneath him. Tettius ran to the pit, not believing what he saw.

With his cock still at full erection, Ammatas somehow was able to direct the fluid where he wanted it to go. The scrotum clinched to point the penis forward, back and side to side, slowly dousing the heat below him with a never ending flow. This amazing organ was used as though it was a massive, pressurized hose and the sounds of hissing, coupled with steam rising from the pit only further dramatized the scene.

Minutes seemed to pass before the gusher began to subside, but not before his mission was accomplished – Ammatas had successfully doused most of the hot coals beneath him, bringing relief to his baked torso.

Tettius felt slightly threatened by this performance from the cross. He wondered how a man could control the penis with such accuracy and instant response, but eventually he shook himself back to reality and regained control of the dungeon. He ordered both prisoners released from their restraints, knowing that other measures would be required. Both prisoners had incredible skills involving their physiques, feats that defied explanation, but Tettius was resolved and challenged to use all the knowledge and trickery he possessed to break these men down.

Preparations were made for a new approach.

Part Five – The Invasion

As the prisoners were brought down from their suspension, Tettius and Emascus spoke privately to one another. A strategy was devised and Tettius decided which brother would be put into which position, "Ammatas on top."

Emascus instructed his guards what to do. As they sprang into action, a loud banging was heard on the door atop the stairs and after a few seconds, one of the guards reported to Tettius.

"A message from the slope, sir."

The commander opened and read the information.

Tettius Fuscus:

3 of the crucified men have died. 1 remains. None confessed. 1 heard to say "Sargenta" just before expiring.

He turned and handed the paper to Emascus, "Sargenta – Do they mean Sergetia? The river?"

"Yes. It flows just outside their fortress walls."

"Of course, the river bed!"

He turned to the guard. "Send a dispatch to Trajanian. Dacian gold is buried in the Sergetia River near the fortress at Sarmizegetuza."

As the guard left the room, Tettius placed his hand onto his comrade's shoulder. "Halfway done, my friend. Now, we go for the old man."

During this event, the Cuspin Guard made ready for the next one.

For Telum, a rounded wooden table sat in wait. The surface was ten feet in diameter and rested three feet from the floor. He was made to lay on his back and spread eagle atop the table, then bound by rope around his ankles and wrists.

His body was stretched taut, but only tight enough to bring slight pain. Each opposite end of the four ropes binding him was threaded into individual hand cranks bolted to the edge of the wood surface. Around the table, these cranks secured the ropes for the prisoner's right hand, right foot, left hand and left foot. Once the man was bound, each crank could be turned to increase or lessen his stretching and then locked into place, keeping him at the desired tension.

As for Ammatas, his wrists were bound together with a chain, which was then placed onto a metal hook. Another chain held the hook and ran to a pulley near the ceiling, where it continued back down to a side wall crank. As it was turned, the arms of Ammatas raised over his head, continuing until he was lifted off the floor. This is when the angle of the overhead chain swung him over the table, while his body continued upwards towards the ceiling.

Once the desired height was obtained, two guards climbed onto the table with the ends of two chains in hand. They wrapped one around his left knee and another around the right, then fastened the final links to the wrapping with clamps. Both guards then exited the top of the table.

The other ends of each of these chains also ran to pulleys at the ceiling, continuing from there back down to side wall cranks. When these were turned, the angle of the chains took the man's legs in opposite directions, forcing him to turn his knees to the outside. The end result: he was suspended vertically above his brother Telum, who was stretched horizontally and spread eagle on the table below. The man above was hanging with wrists locked together and overhead, while the legs were spread wide apart, the knees bent at 75 degree angles and feet dangling with arches turned forward. The distance between the right foot of Ammatas and chest of Telum was three feet and the brothers were perpendicular to each other, vertical above, horizontal below.

Both men were exhausted from their test of strength. Their skin was gritty from layers of dried sweat and Tettius did not care for the odor. "They must be washed of this filth. Bring soap and buckets of water. Use the brushes."

Ladders were placed behind Ammatas and soon both brothers were drenched in soapy water, while horsehair brushes scrubbed their skin. Tettius dipped a cup into one bucket of rinse water and climbed onto the table, bringing with him a three step ladder. He raised himself and the cup for Ammatas to drink. Coming off the ladder, he knelt down to offer fresh water to Telum, but found the strong man fast asleep. Laying horizontal while being soothingly massaged with soapy brushes had instantly put him out.

Tettius smiled at this scene. No wonder the man had collapsed into slumber after his incredible performance of strength and endurance. The interrogator left him to snooze. He wanted this man fully rested for what was to come.

The guards thoroughly and gently cleaned every part of the bound men, including the feet, hair, faces and genitals. Many times before they had done this and they knew what their commander desired of them.

Exiting the table, Tettius signaled the guards to rinse the man above, then the man below. He noticed that Ammatas had also drifted away to snooze, despite his rather uncomfortable suspension.

"Emascus, I am hungry. We will eat here and let them recuperate awhile."

Food and drink was ordered to be brought into the dungeon. Tettius and the Cuspin Guard sat about the room and filled their bellies, while watching the prisoners slumber.

After the servants cleared the room, Emascus retrieved a six step ladder, then a wooden mallet and peculiar device from a shelf on one of the side walls.

Tettius hopped onto the table and gingerly stepped around the slumbering man bound to it. As the guards gathered around to watch, he placed his hands onto the inner thighs of Ammatas, who also slept with chin resting on his chest. Emascus climbed the ladder and inserted the end of his strange device between the butt cheeks of the suspended man, then put the mallet to the other end. With one whack, the instrument entered the prisoner's wide open rectum.

Ammatas was jolted from his sleep and immediately howled in shock, which awakened Telum below.

Straining against his ropes, he cried out, "What are you doing to him?"

With another strike from the mallet, Emascus drove the device deeper into his victim. Made of smoothed wood, this cruel instrument was a butt plug. The total length was seven inches and at the point of insertion, the diameter was one inch, but with each inch of length, the diameter increased by one quarter of an inch. So, the other end of the plug was two and one half inches wide. With only two strikes, the device already was one third of the way inserted into the prisoner's ass.

Ammatas continued to moan from this agonizing invasion, while Telum protested from below, "You sick bastards. What is wrong with you?"

Tettius looked down, while still holding Ammatas steady, "This is a torture chamber... remember? If you want us to stop, you know what you must do."

"It is not torture. It is rape, you sadistic animal."

Ammatas was too stunned and racked with pain to utter any words. With his legs spread wide apart and bent at the knees, the anus was stretched open and completely vulnerable. This first time entry into his virgin ass sent shudders throughout his suspended body and to further add to his pain and humiliation, the foreign object inside him made contact with the prostate gland, bringing an unwanted erection.

Tettius had a close-up view, as the engorged cock protruded just below his eyelevel. He marveled at its intimidating length and thickness for a few seconds, then took the pulsating organ into his hand and mocked its owner. "We've seen your hose douse the fire, soon we will see what else it can do."

He teased the victim by flicking his tongue onto the sensitive skin beneath the head, watching with amazement as the pole sprang upwards to nearly strike its owner's belly. He lightly scratched the man's dangling testicles, then addressed his assistant. "Come, Emascus, let us concentrate on the other, while this one learns to accept what is inside him."

As the final word left his mouth, a mighty salvo of semen spewed from the elongated cock, spattering all over the Roman's face.

"Damn it to hell." He violently wiped the offending cum from his nose and mouth, while a second spurt peppered his chest. "What kind of man are you? No man can control his penis this way."

Despite his agony and degradation, Ammatas forced a smile. For the second time of the interrogation, his amazing tool had been turned into a weapon used to intimidate his tormentor – another small victory gained.

"Come, Emascus, this one is waiting."

Telum was straining with all his might to break free, but the guards who had circled around the table made sure the ropes held firm. The sight of this only further excited Tettius and Emascus. The massive chest rose into the air, while the belly dropped off the end of the rib cage. All muscles in the legs and arms ballooned to incredible thickness and just as before, the bound man appeared not as a mortal, but as a god. He immediately was transformed into a divine hero, a glorious design of masculine strength for all to see. It was there for them, exposed and vulnerable, inviting torment.

"There is no escape for you," Tettius taunted, "Struggle all you like. Your body belongs to us and we will take full advantage."

Realizing the effort was useless, Telum collapsed onto the table, exhausted. With chest and belly heaving, he awaited the assault. "Rack me if you must. I will never talk."

This statement of defiance nearly melted the Roman interrogator, but he had no intention of stretching this man. Although the table was designed to rip apart joints, muscle and tissue, Tettius would use it only for restraint. The torture would come from tongues and lips.

Each man was assigned a body part, but would wait for their signal to begin. It started with the feet. One took the left and the other the right and put their tongues onto the man on the rack. Up and down the soles and in between the toes, the strong arched and manly feet of the prisoner were slimed with spit. He looked up over his chest to witness this torment, groaned and returned his head to the table. The slavish worship affected him in an unexpected way, as a slight rumbling began to stir at his groin, but he quickly turned his thoughts to disgust and thwarted these feelings.

"You bastard. Call them off."

Tettius did not respond to this, but instead put two more to work. They buried their faces into the stretched open arm pits and began to saturate the thick, bushy hairs. Before Telum could react, two more put their tongues to his calves and shins.

He lifted his head and violently lunged at one of the pit men, but the target was out of reach. Defeated, he lowered his head and closed the eyes. Again, the praise lavished upon him stirred his masculinity, but he changed focus.

"This is sick. I'd rather you torture me."

Still no response came from Tettius. Pointing to the chest, two more guards joined the fray and Telum felt tongues on his nipples. He groaned from this degradation.

"No... not that. Make them stop."

Stretched into a perfectly round shape, the manly nipples were ruthlessly assaulted. The combination of wet and sandpaper like stimulation caused the tips to rise and become erect, while another new emotion entered into Telum's brain. Incredible feelings of manliness began to consume him with an intensity he could not suppress. As two more men started their tongue worship on his massive thighs, Telum began to lose control of his thoughts.

He did not realize it, but he started flexing in a pose of masculine beauty. He sucked in and further flattened the belly, while expanding and raising his mighty chest, inviting the tantalizing stimulation of the nipples. His penis quickly filled with blood and awakened, soon flipping onto his belly to throb and bounce. He became so enraptured that he failed to notice when Emascus began to lick and kiss his powerful abdomen, but once he realized another tongue had joined the fray, his cock grew to new strength.

With eyes closed, Telum fell into a near dream state. He flexed and writhed to absorb the incredible praise lavished on him. The back arched and he strained against the ropes, fantasizing that he was the same heroic and manly god that the Romans in reality saw him to be. And then, he was elevated to a higher level of ecstasy, as Tettius placed his tongue onto the reverberating testicles.

Telum recoiled, then relaxed to absorb this glorious stimulation. His toes were curled back, as he exposed the soles of his feet to the amazing tongue worship. Manly ooze dribbled from his slit onto the belly, where Emascus continued to saturate the rock hard surface. Then, just when he thought the level of ecstatic pleasure could get no higher, Telum felt heaven. The mouth of Tettius engulfed him.

With a mighty groan, Telum arched his back and expanded every muscle. Tettius slavishly worshiped the engorged cock, while the bound man writhed and flexed his magnificent form.

Eleven tongues simultaneously enveloped him, while the mouth of Tettius properly serviced his manly phallus. Testosterone raged throughout his body. Every form of stimulation he had secretly desired to give himself was now being given to him by the Romans. This intense oral praise became something indescribable – an otherworldly state that took him beyond the torture rack, beyond the world he knew. His thoughts were no longer under his control and all revulsion towards his tormentors disappeared.

Reverberations rumbled in his groin, as the bulbous nuts began to contract. Then, in a split second, the mouth left him and he heard the word, "STOP!"

All tongues were removed and Telum was abandoned, causing him to cry out in anguish.

"NO! You can't. Why did you stop?"

With a sinister laugh, Tettius revealed the plot. "Not until you talk."

"No, please... you must finish me."

"We are not ready. Tell me about your father, then we will finish you."

"Please... please don't make me. Don't do this."

Tettius crawled onto the flattened belly with his knees and looked down into the eyes of his prisoner.

"You will shoot when I say, not before. How does it feel to have your entire body exploited? You belong to us. Your manhood is ours. Talk and we will give it back to you."

"No... I can't... please finish me."

"You know my answer."

Tettius ordered the tongues to return, but left the tortured penis unattended. Telum writhed in agony, knowing full well that orgasm would not be allowed. His cock bobbed up off the belly with a string of silky pre cum attached. It bounced on the surface in a frenetic dance, as eleven wet tongues worked him over.

"Please... I can't... take this."

Tettius did take him. Again he orally stroked the mighty phallus to the brink of orgasm, then released it and ordered the tongues away.

"Oh, god... NO! Finish me."

"Only you can stop this. Talk and I will finish you."

Telum was nearly in tears. Never in his wildest imagination could he have envisioned such torture. He had mentally prepared himself for enormous amounts of pain, but not this. His enormously muscular physique could not help him now. This was an assault on his manhood, his psyche, his very being.

For the third time, Tettius took the victim's cock deep into the back of his throat, holding it there and squeezing with all his might. Slowly, he withdrew his mouth up the long pole, frantically scraping the underside with his tongue. Again he sensed the organ reverberate in preparation to explode and immediately released it.

"Why? How can you do this to me?"

"Talk and I will finish this."

With a groan, Telum turned the head and closed his eyes, fully realizing his fate. The choice was clear: give in and talk or lie there to suffer the torture of denial.

The pattern was established. Repeatedly, he was stimulated by tongues until the cock was ready. Each time it was prepared to fire, all praise stopped and the interrogation renewed.

Countless times they did this to him and each time his pleadings for release were denied. Brought to the brink again and again, Telum felt as though his scrotum would explode, but still he would not give in. The test of wills pushed him to the limits of sanity, yet somehow he remained defiant.

The poor man was so close to breaking that Tettius could almost taste victory – but just at that moment, help arrived.

As Tettius knelt between the thighs and bent over to service the cock for the umpteenth time, something warm and wet dripped onto the back of his head. He released the tool in his mouth and raised up to see Ammatas firing another round of cum. Touching the back of his head, Tettius looked at the sticky goo on his fingers, then back to the organ that fired it. The damn thing was pointing straight down to target him.

Tettius crushed the sperm into his fist and shook it at the suspended man. "I knew I should have paid more attention to you. Jealous? Is that it? Very well. I will take care of you right now."

Tettius leapt from the table and shouted with rage, "Emascus, the spear."

While Telum lay groaning with scrotum ready to explode, Emascus retrieved another wooden object from the side wall. This implement looked similar to a javelin four and one half feet long, but one end was rounded and three-quarter of an inch in diameter, while the other end tapered to a rounded point of one quarter of an inch.

Emascus took the small end of this javelin and set it into the center of Telum's lower belly, just above the pelvic bone. The exposed end of Ammatas' butt plug contained a hole bored into the center, which just happened to be the perfect diameter to accept the other end of the javelin.

Emascus grabbed the plug and forced it to a vertical position, then inserted the wooden spear into the hole.

Ammatas grunted from the magnified pain of the butt plug inside him. This new angle increased the pressure to the backside of the rectal wall and the javelin forced the plug deeper into him by one quarter of an inch. Below, Telum flexed the arms, expanded the chest and sucked in his belly, lifting his head to see the pointed stick inserted into the muscle. Returning his head to the table, he let out a pitiful moan, fully realizing what was about to happen.

Emascus held the spear in place with his hand gripping the center, while Tettius rose to his feet, standing on the table to glare up at Ammatas. "This will not be pleasant for you. Perhaps you should talk now, before I am forced to further degrade you."

"You can go to hell."

"Probably, but I need the information first. This is your last chance." He grabbed the man's powerful cock and squeezed the shaft. "Where is your father?"

Without warning, another little spurt of cum shot from the slit, striking Tettius just below the mouth and spattering his chin.

He released the penis from his hand and recoiled, "Very clever, my friend." He wiped away the warm semen, pretending to be unaffected by the mysterious ability of Ammatas to use his cock this way. "It will do you no good. One of you will talk... and soon."

Exiting the table, he shouted, "Lower him."

With one turn of the side wall crank, the overhead chain allowed gravity to drop Ammatas one full inch.

Simultaneous groans of horror and agony echoed from the man above and the man below. Telum felt reverberations from his abdomen to groin, as the full weight of his brother drove the spear deep into his belly. At the same time, Ammatas felt an implosion building throughout his rectum, as the butt plug rammed its way further and wider into him.

Testing the tension of the spear, Emascus was satisfied of it being securely in place and removed his hand. The double impalement had begun – one through the rectum and one into the belly. Each man emitted ungodly grunts and groans with every exhale of breath, as their bodies writhed and contorted as much as the bindings would allow. Telum sucked in the belly, vainly trying to alleviate the pressure from him, while Ammatas strained on the overhead chain, uselessly trying to lift himself higher.

Now, the interrogation was intensified. Tettius climbed between the thighs and knelt before the strong man. "Talk, damn you. No man can take this. Neither of you can."

"No... never."

"This has only begun. Do not force me to make it worse. Talk now."

Mighty groans and grunts rumbled from his chest, as he flattened the belly to the table, but still he shook his head 'no'.

"Again."

Another revolution of the crank further impaled both victims, bringing forth unholy cries of unbridled pain and humiliation. The plug was now completely buried into the suspended man's ass. Two and one-half inches ripped Ammatas open, while the length of the foul object penetrated to the highest point of his rectal wall.

Shockwaves of agony reverberated throughout the abdomen of Telum. The spear impaled his muscle deep, seeming to nearly run him through. This also sent shocks throughout his groin, causing the thick cock to remain fully engorged, violently bobbing and bouncing into the air, then back down to his belly.

Tettius ordered the guards to resume orally desecrating Telum's powerful form, leaving his writhing penis unattended to further torment and punish him. Springing to his feet, Tettius focused his pressure on Ammatas. "What about you? Will you talk?"

"Never."

"You've seen what I can do. Do you want me to rupture you?"

"It is your decision."

Returning to his knees, Tettius resumed tormenting the man on the rack. He ruthlessly sucked the hardened cock, while the victim writhed in agony and ecstasy. Brought to the edge, Telum was once more denied his orgasm.

"Oh, my god...not again."

"All day, until you talk. One of you will tell me."

Tettius again took the organ into his mouth, while the guards slimed the rest of Telum's body. The Roman ruthlessly stroked up and down to further torture the cock, but was interrupted by a drenching on the back of his head. Letting go with the mouth, he jolted back to see another stream of urine flowing from the penis above, which again was pointing straight down to aim at where he had been.

Tettius watched in horror, as the stream flooded Telum's throbbing cock. Then, with a sudden clinching of the scrotum and twisting of the pelvis, Ammatas targeted the final drops towards the Roman, striking him on the thigh with foul-smelling piss. The face turned red and eyes became crazed with anger. For the first time in his storied and successful career as the Empire's premier interrogator, Tettius

Fuscus forgot his purpose. His authority had been challenged by this man's phallic weapon and this he would not tolerate.

"Damn it, I will subdue this foul penis once and for all. Heat a skewer and bring it to me."

A guard placed one end of a long, metal pin into the fire, then brought it to the table. Taking the skewer, Tettius grabbed the hardened cock by its head and forced open the slit, still dribbling the remnants of yellow urine. He inserted the pointed pin and pushed downward, driving the skewer from the slit and through the underside of the cock head.

Unholy cries of pain and sadness pierced the air, as the magnificent penis was ruthlessly mutilated. Telum was not sure exactly what was happening, but knew from the voice of his brother it was something horrendous. These were sounds he had never before heard and the astonished expressions on the faces of the Cuspin Guard and Emascus told him an awful event had taken place.

Emascus was particularly perplexed. He sensed that his friend might be drifting into dangerous territory, but his loyalty told him to remain firm and wait to see where this was going. He climbed onto the table and positioned himself so that Telum could not see what was happening.

Like a madman, Tettius leapt from the table and ran to his clothing piled on the floor. Reaching into the mess, he produced a gold ring and returned to the suspended prisoner. "This I took from another prisoner long ago. He was Nubian and wore this on his ear. Look, Ammatas, see how it opens?"

He glanced down at his bloodied cock, but could bear to look no more, thrusting his head back with a moan of anguish.

Tettias inserted the ring, locked and turned it so the connection was buried into the meat of the cock head. "There, now you are subdued. Now I will lead you about like a beast, because that is what you are."

He jumped off the table and picked up a club from the side wall. This club had a short chain and hook attached to one end and Tettius swung the chain with menacing authority. "Remove that plug and bring him to me. Bind the wrists behind him."

As guards turned the cranks to raise Ammatas, Emascus held the butt plug until it slipped out of the rectum, then tossed it and the spear to the floor. The chains around his knees were loosened and removed, then they swung Ammatas away from the table and brought him down.

Two guards unwrapped the chain from his wrists, then held him up and bound the wrists behind his back with rope, while Tettius hooked his club through the ring hanging from the end of his cock. "Come with me, dog. I have another surprise for you." Leading with his custom-made leash, Tettius pulled his prisoner towards the pit of fire. Once there, he ordered the guards to hold Ammatas steady, while he grabbed another skewer.

Taking the left nipple between finger and thumb, Tettius stretched the skin away from the body and gave his victim another piercing. Another ungodly howl shook the walls of the dungeon, as the crazed Roman mercilessly mutilated another body part. Soon, another gold ring was produced and attached to the poor man's nipple.

"Now I have my choice. I can lead you around from the cock or the tit, whichever strikes my fancy."

And this is exactly what he did. Ammatas was forced to parade about the floor of the dungeon, as Tettius cruelly tugged on his cock with the leash. As they passed by the table where Telum lay, Emascus again blocked his view, "Don't look, it is too horrible. I fear Tettius has gone mad. Give me time. Somehow I will stop this."

He waited for the prisoner and his tormentor to pass and parade toward the far end of the dungeon, then got a reading from the rest of the Cuspin Guard. He moved from one to the other, whispering to them that Tettius had gone too far and must be stopped. The look on each man's eyes told him they were on his side and he returned to Telum. "We are one. We will save your brother, but don't make a move until we do."

Quietly, each crank was turned to lessen the tension of ropes. Telum did not know what had happened, but sensed that Emascus was sincere and could be trusted. Considering the alternative was continued torture, he followed the Roman's instruction and remained quietly laying spread eagle on the table.

Longtime friends, Emascus felt it was his duty to allow Tettius to redeem himself. As he and Ammatas made the corner by the pee hole and turned around to head back to the center of the room, Tettius found his friend blocking the path.

"Look Emascus. See my new dog?"

"Tettius, you must stop. You have gone too far."

"You are weak, Emascus. Why don't you go back where you belong and leave me be. Maybe you can think of something to do with that other Dacian beast."

Emascus knew he had lost his friend. Wild eyes and frothing mouth told him all he needed to know, but still he gave the man one last chance.

"This is beneath us. We are Romans, Tettius. You must remember this."

"Get out of my way, traitor."

He shoved Emascus aside and continued the humiliating procession. Ammatas could barely stand, weakened as he was from endless hours of torture, but he bravely followed the leash, straining to keep up with its holder. As Tettius approached the center of the room, Emascus gave the order and the Cuspin Guard pounced upon the crazed man, forcing him to release the club. He was immediately subdued and bound with rope around the chest and arms.

Ammatas collapsed to the floor, where several guards removed the leash and tended to him. As for Telum, once he saw the rings he violently struggled to break free. The anger brought him newfound strength and he severed the bindings on his wrists, quickly rising to sit on the table. Emascus tried to calm him.

"Telum, you and your brother will be tortured no more. When Trajanian returns, all will be resolved. His strict orders were that no harm should come to either of you and Tettius has disobeyed the Emperor's wishes. I have taken charge in order to ensure your safety and recovery from what has happened. You must trust me. Do not force me to put you in chains again."

For reasons he could not fully explain, Telum did trust this man. Perhaps it was the genuine admiration he had felt from this Roman when his oral worship was performed near the pit. What was clear to him was that Emascus had proven his sincerity by stopping the sadistic cruelty of a madman, just as he had promised.

"I will not fight you. I trust you to do what is right by me and my brother."

The ropes were removed from his ankles, but Telum did not strike out towards the Romans. His only concern was to comfort Ammatas and two guards escorted him in that direction – not as a prisoner, but as a friend whose weakened state required their assistance.

Emascus now ended all doubt of his good intentions. "You two at the door, unlock it and send word to the slope. The crucified man is to be released immediately."

"That prisoner is no more, sir."

"When did this happen."

"Word just came moments ago."

Moisture formed in the corner of one eye, but this sad news only strengthened the resolve of Emascus and furthered his anger towards the fallen Roman, Tettius.

"Tettius Fuscus, I am charging you with high treason against Rome and the Emperor Trajanian. You will be locked into a cell until the Emperor returns. Then, you will have your say."

With a crazed, nearly nonhuman cackle, Tettius lashed out, "Oh, no... not me. You're the traitor... not me. Your head will be served on a platter... not me. You're the one..."

"Enough!" Emascus motioned to the guards. "Take him."

Tettius was led screaming out of the dungeon and locked into a holding cell, still bound with rope. Emascus and the remaining guard lifted poor Ammatas to his feet, then guided him and his brother towards the stairwell.

"We will take you for medical treatment, Ammatas. The rings will be removed and your wounds will be healed in time. We will await the return of Trajanian and I will speak on your behalf. You both are now my responsibility."

Part Six – All the Gold for the Emperor

Trajanian did return next day and brought with him Decebalus, King of Dacia. Upon hearing of the sadistic mutilation in the torture chamber, the Emperor summoned Tettius and could quickly see that the man's mind no longer belonged to him.

No mercy was given, with the exception that Tettius was allowed to choose – he could die like a Roman or take his own life.

By the time his execution took place, Tettius Fuscus was a blathering idiot, screaming out meaningless blurbs about poisonous semen and other nonsense up to the moment a tribune's sword pierced into his gut.

Agreements were made for the future alliance of Rome and Dacia. Trajanian kept his gold and other treasures taken from the river bed, while King Decebalus gifted to him the sleek and chiseled, youthful firebrand Ammatas, his son. He returned to Rome with the Emperor and was always by his side. Trajanian learned first hand the incredible skills possessed by this Dacian prince and came to love this human treasure far more than what had been plucked from the River Sergetia.

In exchange, Dacia became a Roman province with King Decebalus as governor. Using their engineering expertise, the Romans rebuilt what had been destroyed during the siege of Sarmizegetuza and sent a special envoy to establish the new government. This duty was given to Emascus. He was appointed by Trajanian to oversee all reconstruction and protection of the city, a function which required much of his time. Even so, Emascus somehow managed to frequently visit his newfound friend, Telum.

The powerfully masculine Dacian warrior discovered that he always looked forward to these private visits, as he was lavished with the attention only Emascus could give him. The bonds between the two men became unbreakable and all resentments were put aside – all misdeeds forgiven. Soon, the horrid memories faded for Telum and Emascus. Their experiences together took them to places far away from the torture chamber of one Tettius Fuscus.

ABOUT THE AUTHOR

Jardonn Smith is the instigator of the BDSM web site Jardonn's Erotic Tales. He writes fiction derived from his boyhood inspirations, fantasies concocted from any film or television program he saw that depicted men shirtless, bound and interrogated. As he says, "The male physique is undoubtedly handsome, but put it on a stretch rack or a cross and it becomes glorious."

This is his first collection of published short stories. He lives in a house with a cat named Bud, much tobacco and much coffee.

www.ingramcontent.com/pod-product-compliance
Lightning Source LLC
Chambersburg PA
CBHW071221260626
47162CB00004B/1382